AF612531

RETURN TO THE UNCANNY

DORIAN J. SINNOTT

All works included in this anthology are reprints from their original publications, who own first time publication rights. Permission was granted prior to the release of this anthology.

A SINNOTT ART STUDIO PUBLICATION

Cover illustration and cover layout by BetiBup33
Interior illustrations by Belinda Sinnott, Mark Sinnott, and Joe Sinnott

Library of Congress Cataloging-in Publication Data

Sinnott, Dorian J.

Sinnott Art Studio

ISBN: 979-8-706-71162-7

Printed in the United States of America

10 9 8 7 6 5 4 3 2 1

In Memory of Joe Sinnott

who loved these dark tales…

My Poppy. My Muse. My Hero.

JOE SINNOTT '19

TABLE OF CONTENTS

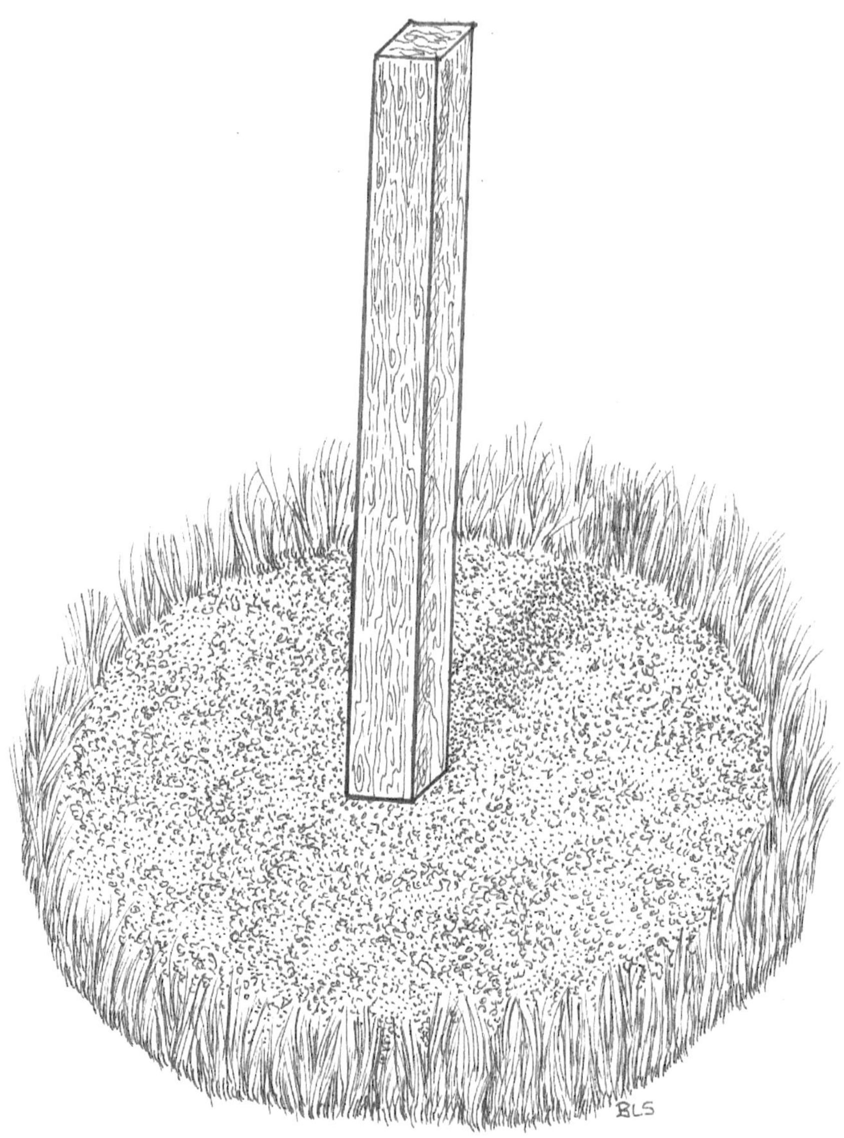
BLS

The Post

Published in Nightingale & Sparrow (2019)

I'll never forget that post at the far end of the field. It was old and rotted, wood splintered from years of weathering. Father said they used to tie horses to it after the plows returned at dusk. But we never saw any plows. Nor any horses. All we saw was the post, and the circle of dirt around it where no grass ever grew.

I was only seven when the Fitch family agreed to take us. I'll admit, I was terrified at first. The gray, dreary orphanage had become so homey over the years, and looking back, it was all I had come to know. But for you, I know it was different. You were nearly twice my age, and memories of a world outside the walls still were fresh. You longed for freedom. All of us did. But there was something about the farms and the fields that brought fear to my young heart. There were no street lights there, no cars, no people. It was nothing like our temporary home in the city. On the farms, there was nothing but darkness. Silence.

On our first night in the Fitch home, I remember that silence. The stillness. There was no laughter from other children, no sirens in the distance. And there was no you. For the last three years, after the caregivers had turned us in for the night, you'd always let me sneak into your bed. But now, for the first time, I had been alone.

Your bedroom was on the opposite end of the farm house, and the lack of light kept me from venturing the halls. The shadows were far thicker than in the city, heavy and foul. Endless. For the first few months, you'd tell me there was nothing to be afraid of in them. That shadows thrived out in the country. No different than flickering office lights overnight in the city. But I still was convinced otherwise.

There are shadows in the halls, I'd tell you. *Ghosts in the walls*.

Yet, the only one in time that I know you came to believe, was the monster.

There's a monster in Father's heart.

Before we came along, Fitch lived alone. He was a widower – his wife and young son passing from what he claimed was illness years before. He was always so quiet. Sullen. You told me it was his grief. That having children in the house again most likely reminded him of his life before. Perhaps even of his own son. And so, I know you tried. Tried with every bit of your might to comfort him. To please him. But the kindness was never returned.

Fitch made it clear to us that we were merely coming to live on his farm as extra hands—*workers*. He said the crops were full in the summer, and by winter, you'd be strong enough to do chores and manual labor. Me, on the other hand, he had time to wait on. And so, for that first summer, from sunrise to sunset, you'd be in the fields. Watching. Learning.

At first, you didn't mind the chores. But as soon as autumn began to rear its head on the crest of dying summer, so did the beast. Fitch's stone-like exterior grew darker. More gruff. And that's when the shadows felt heavier on the house than before.

I noticed only a few at first, hidden under the sleeves of your flannel shirt. But as the weeks went on, your bruises became darker. Deeper. And there were more than just on your arms. I spotted them on your back when you undressed in the late evening. And on your cheek. You'd always been the stronger of us—after all, you were the big brother. But, I remember the tears. You tried so hard to hide them behind your puffy and irritated eyes. Pain poured out when it couldn't withstand any longer. And so did heartbreak.

Even when there were no more crops to tend to as autumn began to fade into dreary winter, Father would have you in the fields. Learning. I'd watch from the frost covered windows. He'd stand over you, barking orders, having you dig. The frozen earth wouldn't budge as easy as it had in the summer, and your cracked and blistered hands trembled with every attempt you made. And you had no coat. Only your thinly worn out flannel shirt was left to cover you as you drove the shovel harder to the ground. I could see the tears pricking at your eyes again, even from behind the glass. But, with every failed attempt, Father would only get more impatient. More angry. I shielded my eyes when his demands became louder, and he grabbed your shoulders.

I managed the courage one night to slip into your room. Through the shadows and past the door to Father's room. We knew he was usually fast asleep once the last light of day had vanished. A bottle of gin usually helped with that. I remember sitting at the foot of your bed that night, watching you with weary eyes. I wanted nothing more than to be away from the farm. To be back in the bleak orphanage.

"It's not Father's fault, Freddie." Your words were soft. "I know he's sad. He drinks. It's not his fault. I… I just need to work harder."

"But there are shadows," I'd say again. "Shadows in the halls. Ghosts in the walls… And there's a monster—"

"I know," you'd say. "A monster in Father's heart."

You shifted under the covers, wincing from the marks left behind by your lessons. With a sigh, you glanced back at me before ushering me to my room.

"It's called grief. That monster. He misses his wife. His son…"

I stopped in the doorway. "Bill… is he ever going to, *actually* adopt us?"

"Next summer, maybe. We just have to work hard."

Every day as autumn faded, you were back outside—digging. I'd grown tired of watching from the window. I knew the routine well. It was always the same. You'd struggle with the shovel, barely breaking the frozen dirt beneath you. And then the words would begin. The shouting. The lashing.

It took until the first week of December for you to dig the hole as wide and deep as Father wanted it.

For a few days after that, the chores stopped. Father retired to his room and only made himself known for dinner. We spent the days together, like we used to, playing board games and laughing over old memories. That was the first I'd seen you smile in months.

But your smile quickly vanished just as soon as it had returned. You came to my room one afternoon, pale, with a look of dread on your face. I remember asking what was wrong. *Are you sick*? You told me we needed to leave. Back to the orphanage—*anywhere*.

I didn't physically ask why. I didn't get a chance to. You tossed a box of photos on my bed, silent. When I asked where you found them, all you could muster was, "wall".

Ghosts.

I fingered through them, carefully taking note of what they were of. Children. So many children. About the age of you. All the photos weren't on the farm, however. They were photos taken at various orphanages and children's homes. All children taken in for "work". But, what caught my attention was the fact that they all had been crossed out. Thick, black marker struck across their faces. As if they were unworthy. Forgotten.

"W-where are…?"

I didn't know how to finish my sentence. Even at a young age, I knew very well what was going on. It was then my fingers stopped on the final photograph. The photo of Fitch's wife and young son. The marks were old, but the ink still dark and thick across their faces. Thicker than any of the others.

You wasted no time in gathering a few items in a knapsack, waiting for dusk. At first, you told me to stay and wait, that you'd be back with help. But I begged to go with you. I pleaded. When you finally gave in and agreed to let me come along, your plans were foiled.

Father stood in the doorway, having overheard everything you proposed. His eyes were red and irritated, most likely from drinking, and his tone was deep. He called you an ingrate for wanting to run away, after all he had done for you. For *us*. How we never were going to be worthy of being *his* children. How, *no one* had ever been worthy of being *his* children.

I remember him dragging you outside, through the cold night air. He shoved you to the ground before the hole and threw the shovel beside you.

"Dig." Was all he said. "You keep digging until I say you can stop."

And so you did. You dug harder and deeper than ever before. Your calloused hands split open, staining the shovel in a sticky red. But you never stopped. Not until Father watched the sun rise over the fields. And then, he stepped in and yanked the shovel away. I couldn't hear what he said through the tightly shut windows, but he stared at you—so closely—and I saw you flinch.

Once again, I watched as he dragged you, further into the fields. To the post.

Father always told us to never play near the post. He said it wasn't safe, that the ground there was weak and we might fall through. He said, that's why the grass never grew around it. Weak spots.

There were tears rolling down your cheeks as you begged him to forgive you. Yet, Father didn't listen. Using a thick leather, reins from a horse the farm no longer had, he bound your hands to the post. You squirmed and pleaded, wrists burning as the tight binds dug deeper into your skin with each movement you made. Your blood smeared against the wood—and for the first time, you noticed that yours wasn't the only one. The post was more than just withered and splinted. It was stained in blood. Through the cracks. Old, and soiled.

After Father took you to the post, I never saw you again.

He'd told me that you were to stay out there all day, all night, as punishment. That this was the only way you'd learn your lesson. That you'd be strong. Strong for next summer. He told me, when morning came, you would be untied. Free. And so, I waited. I watched out my bedroom window, until the darkness flooded the fields, and there was nothing but blackness to stare back at me.

At dawn, you were gone. The leather reins had been removed, and you were nowhere to be found. Father was up early, making coffee, mixing it with his gin. He didn't speak a word to me, and his expression was stoic. I went into the fields that morning, hoping that you had escaped in the night. That you had cut the reins free and gone to get help like you promised. But in the chill of the winter air, I felt the sting of solitude. And I knew, you weren't coming back.

Father joined me outside not too long after that, with a wooden post in hand. He carried it over to where the hole you had dug the night before was—only now, it was filled back in. He secured the post into the dirt, and then hammered it down, deep, with the shovel. When he finished, he wiped his brow, and looked at me for only a moment.

"Don't play near the post, my boy," he said. "The ground's weak. You might fall through. Couple years' time, I bet the grass won't be growing."

At nightfall, I waited for Father to fall asleep before taking my knapsack and leaving the house. The shadows and darkness were thick as I crossed the field, careful not to tread near the posts, in case the soil dragged me under. I must have been silent, or Father under a heavy gin-induced sleep. He never woke, and he never looked for me.

I traveled as far as I could, before I was picked up by an older couple who told me I looked as though I'd seen the devil. At this point, I'm not sure I hadn't.

It's been almost twenty years, and I've moved back to the city now. I've always felt comfort in those lights and sounds. The shadows are few and far between. I'd read in the papers some time back, that children had gone missing near an old farm. Something about them being found, buried, in mass graves. I tried not to think of it. But, still, sometimes, I stay up late, thinking about *you*. About the cold air that night. About the shadows, the ghosts, and the monster. And I still think about the farm. *Graves*. About Fitch. But, more than anything, about that post. The one at the far end of the field, old and splintered. The one where the grass around it never grew.

The Cat

Published in Forest of Fear Volume 1 (2019)

My sister begged to keep her—that mangy cat we found on our porch a week before Halloween. She insisted she was a good omen, but I teased that she was probably conjured up by witches. Demons. Sent here to steal our breaths. Our souls. Yet, she made herself right at home. Curled up in our bed, purring her little heart away. It was only on Halloween night, after we'd turned in from a late night of Trick 'r Treating that I noticed it. That heavy, foul stench of death. Coming from her. The cat whose eyes now burned red.

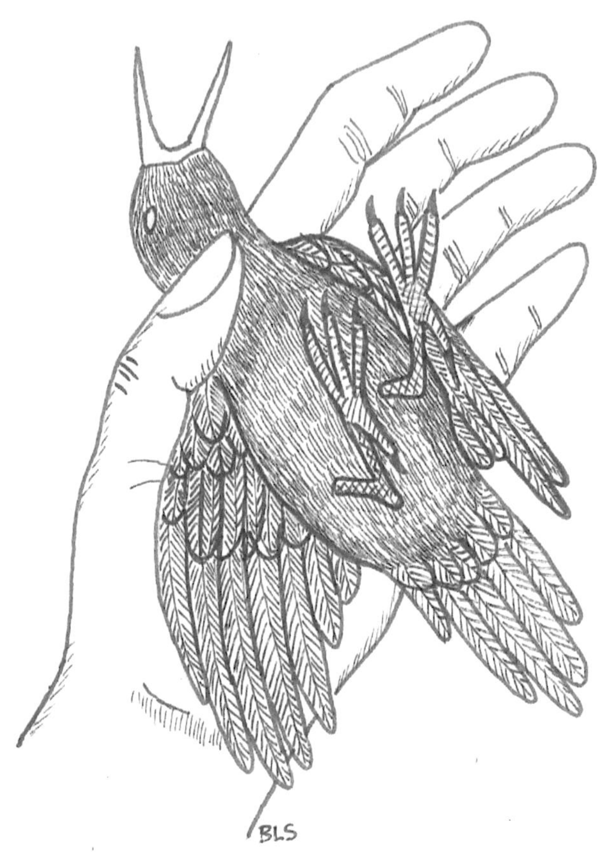
BLS

Liza Crane

Published in Dark Fire Fiction (2020)

There was a girl in our town who said she could bring animals back from the dead. Young Liza Crane. She claimed she did it from time to time in the forest—birds and squirrels. But the townsfolk never believed her. They'd scold her for telling stories, saying that she'd be pegged a "witch". But she never stopped. She insisted that what she said was true, and that she did, indeed, have the gift of rebirth.

It was little Jimmy Carbo who was the first to state her claims were true. Though only eight, he was adamant that Liza could return life to the dead.

"I saw her!" he proclaimed. "A bird hit the window and she brought it back!"

Everyone was convinced the poor creature had simply gone into shock, and recovered. It had *not* come back from the dead. But little Jimmy Carbo still believed what he had saw. And so, word spread through the school house—to the children.

Young minds were much more akin to the idea of "magic", and so, they believed Jimmy, that the stories of Liza were true. So much so, that the day little Mary Bishop's cat died, she carried its lifeless body, wrapped in a blanket, to the porch of Liza Crane. It took longer than it had for the small bird, but without a doubt, Mary heard the corpse in the blanket start to purr.

"You're magic!" she exclaimed. "You brought Cali back!"

Of course, Mary's mother and father still were skeptical. They said Cali was gone, and that the cat they now owned was a replacement. One Liza probably found wandering around—to mend a grieving child's heart. But, that didn't explain the mannerisms, or the little patch of white on the cat's flank, shaped like a heart. It surely did *look* like Cali. And *act* like Cali.

When word got out about the Bishop family's cat, more children began to become intrigued. When their beloved pets passed away, they'd bring her their bodies. And, just like with Cali, one by one, they would be reborn.

The parents still wrote it off as coincidence. They said, animals were easy to replace—especially the small ones. Liza had to have look-alikes she swapped out, claiming she had a gift. But the children argued otherwise. They said they had seen it with their own eyes. The animals that returned home weren't copies. They were, indeed, their beloved pets.

After a few months, however, Liza Crane began to not show herself as often. She'd remain in her house, in the dark, away from the outside world. Children would knock on her door, eagerly awaiting her. But oftentimes, she wouldn't answer.

It was when little Jimmy Carbo's dog passed, when she finally did.

But she looked tired. So worn down and frail. Yet, she agreed to revive the Carbo's dear dog. Only this time, it came with a warning.

"I'm not as well as I used to be," Liza said. "I'm afraid my gift may not be as kind. I can't promise you that this time, your dog will come back as he was. So full of life."

Jimmy didn't argue. He simply begged her to breathe new life into his beloved friend.

"It will take me a few days," Liza said. "But, I promise you that he'll return."

And so, Jimmy trusted her word.

Now was when there were hushed whispers through the streets. The Carbo family had said their dog passed only three days before, but now, there he was. Sitting on their front porch. At first, just like so many of the others, they attempted to write it off as coincidence. That a dog that looked similar to their recently departed had found its way to their porch. But the markings were the same. And the dog knew who they were instantly. And his collar—inscribed with "Rusty" and their address—was around his neck.

Was what Liza claimed true? The question drifted through town. *Maybe she was a witch, after all…*

In a few weeks' time, however, the Carbo family began to notice something off. Their dog mostly laid around, no longer active as he was. And the smell that emanated from him was of decay. They called their vet, reporting his lethargic state and the odor, and were instructed to bring him right in. What they were told, they were unsure if they already knew, or if it was truly shock.

Rusty had no heartbeat.

The vet claimed that his vitals were nonexistent, that it was as if he were a reanimated corpse. It just wasn't possible. Little Jimmy Carbo told his family, once again, that Liza had brought the dog back, that she was *magic*. But, the sense of happiness that their beloved pet had returned wasn't what was delivered. It was fear.

Rusty still laid around, stench growing stronger and harder to bear. He became irritant, as well. Whenever anyone went to pet him, he would turn his jowls up and snarl, exposing rotten gums and mucousy saliva. Jimmy no longer attempted to be near his once faithful friend.

Yet still, no one had seen Liza Crane. She stayed locked away in her house at the end of the street, curtains drawn. A few townsfolk stopped by and knocked, wanting to ask her about the Carbo's dog. If, she had, indeed, been a witch. But she never answered. No matter how many months passed.

It was only when a young girl, Kathy May, stopped by the house, that Liza reappeared. Kathy pounded on the door, sobbing audibly into the evening air. Begging. When Liza finally appeared, she found the young child was holding an infant in her arms.

"Please…" was all the child said.

Kathy May explained that her younger brother had choked on a piece of one of his toys that became dislodged. That she had tried everything. Her parents had stepped outside to grab something for the family for dinner, and she was terrified of what they would say when they came home.

"Please bring Johnny back…"

Liza was hesitant. She explained to Kathy that her gift only worked on animals, and that even now, it was beginning to take its toll on her. She was becoming too weak, too little of her own life. There wasn't enough to spare to revive the infant.

But still, Kathy begged. Pleaded.

The look of desperation in the child's eyes was one that Liza couldn't refuse. With a sigh, she took the lifeless infant from the girl.

"You must give me a few days… but he will return."

Kathy May's family arrived home to find the lifeless body of their son, and their daughter, smiling brightly. They were horrified, sobbing and begging to know what had happened. But, Kathy assured them that everything would be fine.

"He choked… but he'll be okay. Liza is going to bring him back!"

And, sure enough, on the day of the child's funeral, there was a wail from inside the coffin. Baby Johnny had returned. Just as Kathy May had said.

Now, the town was at Liza Crane's door. Pounding at it and demanding to see her. They called her a witch, unsure if blessed or cursed. Yet, no matter how hard and loud they hollered, she never appeared. A few of the men were able to break the door down, searching through the house, for any sign of Liza.

It was only when they reached the master bedroom on the second floor that they found her. Lifeless. Still. Stiff. She looked far older than the young woman she was known to be. As if, only the passing of a few months had been a century. Her eyes were sunken in, skin greyed and pulled tight against the bone. And her once light chestnut hair had fallen a silky white. She was nothing how the townspeople remembered.

On a dreary autumn morning, they laid Liza Crane to rest. Beneath an old oak tree in the cemetery. It wasn't long after, that the children began to claim their pets, once brought back by her gift of life, too, began to perish. First the small ones. And then, little Jimmy Carbo's dog. Kathy May's family was the one who took the effect the hardest, however. They already had to witness the loss of Johnny once—and now a second time. Late in the night.

No one spoke of Liza Crane and her gift after that. Once all the pets and little Johnny were laid to rest. The town claimed that they were believing old stories—that no life had ever been reborn. That, they were just caught up in the childish magic of pretend.

Yet, as soon as early winter arrived and the snow fell hard, the town couldn't deny what they'd seen beneath the old oak in the cemetery. At Liza Crane's grave. There, protruding from the snow, beautiful spring blossoms bloomed. Full of life.

The Watcher

Published in 101 Proof Horror (2020)

I could feel him watching me again. From the corner of my room, deep in the dark shadows, I knew he was there. Staring. Looking on with empty eyes. Eyes I could never see. But I swore I felt them. Fixated so firmly – so stern – never moving from my body nestled in bed. And it was the same every night, like clock-work. Just after the midnight hour.

When the shadows thickened and fell heavy across my room, he would appear. A figure darker than the darkness itself. A void in the never-ending night. The man of midnight. The Watcher.

He was clad in black from head to toe, in a long coat and wide brimmed hat. But I never saw his face. The dense darkness wiped away all traces of distinguishable features. And he never spoke. Not one word. He'd just stand there in the corner, unmoving, yet always watching. Waiting for the dawn to breathe new light into my room, swallowing the shadows.

As I child, he would visit me nightly. It began when I was around six or seven – the ripe age when imagination ran wild. I'd told my mother about him many times over the years of my youth. Asking if she had seen him. Begging her to stay in my room. Leave a light on. But she told me I had been eating too many sweets before bed. Watching too many scary movies. But I knew what I had seen. I felt him there every night. Standing in the corners. In the doorway. Watching. Waiting.

At first, his presence troubled me. The tall shadow man peering into my room from around the open doorway. Gliding in on the darkness of night. Standing just out of the reach of light to look upon me. But in time, after waiting up and being greeted by him nightly, I began to feel at ease with each of his arrivals. What seemed like lonely nights after my family had turned in to sleep weren't as unbearable. I had a friend. A *Watcher*, who came from afar just to visit me.

And so, I'd sit on the edge of my bed, telling him stories of my day and my friends. Of my hopes for the future. My unobtainable, childish dreams. He was always the perfect listener. Never once interrupting, never once interjecting. My words spilled from my lips and bled into the void. The darkness that waited in the corner of my room.

Every night. For three years.

I don't quite remember the exact day it was that the Watcher stopped making visits to my home. It was around early spring, on the eve of my ninth year. The rain had fallen hard through the night, and the distant sound of thunder had kept me up later than usual. I watched the lightning flash from my window, illuminating my room in golden glow.

It wasn't until the rumble of thunder drew closer and I cowered back into my blankets that I saw him, standing in the hall outside my room. He seemed darker than before, the shadows radiating from him drowning any speck of light. Even the lightning deflected from his form, leaving nothing but a solid, black void. I waited, hesitantly, terrified by the constant roaring of thunder that only grew louder. The Watcher, I was convinced, could see my fear. Perhaps for the first time.

Through the shadows, I saw him raise an arm – a long, slender limb, ending in what appeared to be a skeletal hand. He beckoned me from my illuminated bedroom to the darkness of the hallway.

I'd never seen any limbs on the Watcher before. He had merely been a solid figure – a shape in the darkness. Arms glued to his sides. Hidden within his long coat. But on that night, they were clear as day. And their forceful gesture was commanding. To the point my body couldn't resist conforming.

The floor was cold as my bare feet touched it, my movements slow. Looking back, I can't quite recall what made me obey. Perhaps it was my fear of the thunder or simply because he was my friend. Or, maybe, it wasn't even *me* that made the decision at all. But still, I followed. Greeting the Watcher and the darkness in silence.

Just as he had in my room, he remained an immobile figure. Looking up at him, I don't think I realized from a distance just how tall he had been, either. He towered above me, a wall of endless abyss. A darkness that my eyes just couldn't adjust to. I continued gazing up at him, awaiting a reaction. And that was the first time I saw it. The smile that stained his face. That wide, sinister sneer.

My blood went cold.

From the safety of my bed, the Watcher was nothing more than a figure that appeared before me. A simple trick of the light, or lack thereof. But now, standing inches away from him, the feeling of dread overtook me. That feeling I had felt the first night I saw him. Uninvited. Waiting in my doorway to be let in.

The air grew cold and heavy with a stench of sulfur. This wasn't the man I knew. This wasn't my *friend.* Above me, a pair of cat-like yellow eyes gleamed through the darkness. Shining from the light his void had smothered.

I backed away towards my room, but the shadows stopped me. They snaked around my legs like misty tendrils, stinging at the touch. I searched for a sound, but nothing emitted from my throat. I was frozen. Paralyzed. The Watcher approached me, floating almost like a black cloud. His eyes burned in baleful lust, and I could see his arm rising towards me again. It quivered, boney and lanky, aimed for my throat. And that smile. That maniacal, never fading smile…

I found the voice that had been quelled in me. And I screamed.

My mother found me standing in the hallway, covered in a cold sweat and trembling. The hallway was bathed in the light she had turned on, and all she kept asking was what was wrong. Why I was in the hall. Why I had left bed. I told her because of the man. The man in the hat. The Watcher. The stories she had heard so many times over the years. And just like before, she wrote it off as a bad dream. Brought on by the storm. But nevertheless, she let me stay in her room that night. Nestled between her and my father. I didn't sleep a wink. My eyes only focused on the dark corners of her room. The shadows.

That was the last night I saw him. I had finally broke down and begged my mother to buy a nightlight for my room – something to keep the darkness at bay. And though she was hesitant at first, she gave in. To both a small, plug-in nightlight and a set of string lights to outline my window.

From that night forward, my room glistened in soft ambient light. The faint glow stretched across my bed, lighting even the darkest of the corners in amble light. There was nowhere for the Watcher to go now. Nowhere for him to hide. But still, I found myself gazing out into the dark of the hallway at night. Every night. For the rest of my childhood and teenage years.

It's been twenty years since my encounter with the Watcher. Twenty years since I have seen his dark figure haunting my halls. Haunting the corners of my room. But still, I keep a light on in my room – even if small. Just enough to cast faint rays through the shadows. Dispelling the aura of night.

For a long while, I did the same for my daughter, too. I'd bought her colorful string lights to drape over her curtains – illuminating her bedroom window in gentle light. But as she reached her seventh year, she began to complain about the brightness. That it was too much for her to fall asleep to. That she preferred the darkness.

And so, with my wife's coaxing, we removed the string lights from her room.

That's when she started asking about him. About the shadow man. The tall one with the hat and coat. The one that stood in the corner of her room at night. Watching her. My wife laughed it off, saying the same old thing my mother had said to me as a child. But I knew better. I'd seen what she saw. Felt his gaze every night. For those three long years.

"She's not lying," I told my wife. "The man in the hat… the Watcher… I used to see him, too."

I went on to tell her about the countless nights he would appear to me. Standing just out of reach, waiting until the light of morning touched the room – whisking him away in a shroud of smoke. I told her how he stared with those empty voids. Eyes that couldn't be seen, but felt. And then, I told her about that night. The night he lured me from my bed. The night I saw his features – clear as day.

"What does it want?" my wife asked.

I wish I could have had an answer for her. I had speculation – all of which were things I knew she didn't want to hear. But instead, I offered the only advice I had. The only thing that I knew would keep him away. Out of our daughter's room.

"We need to turn her lights back on," I said.

That night, I plugged in her string lights and let their glow cover the room. I watched as my daughter blinked back their glow, but I assured her that they would keep the monsters away. Keep *him* away. I even went as far as to bring the nightlight from our bedroom in. Plug it into the socket in the corner. Eliminating any chance of shadow or darkness that he could find.

"He can't find you now," I said. "He's afraid of the light. And as long as you keep those lit, he can't come in here."

I planted a kiss on my daughter's forehead and turned out the overhead light for the night. The soft colorful glow of her room lit up the hallway as I departed, bidding her sweet dreams.

For about a week, all had been well. She stopped speaking of the Watcher and was back to her cheery self. But I'd began to notice how tired I was becoming. Drained. As though I hadn't caught an ounce of sleep. But I was certain that I had. Though I knew I'd been tossing and turning more through the night – worried about my daughter – I hadn't been awake. At least, I didn't *think* I had been. But when the shadows began to stir again in the corners of my room, I knew all I needed to.

He was back. And I'd felt him watching. Preventing me from sleep.

This time, however, it wasn't from the corners that I saw him. It was at the edge of my bed. Looming over me. Just as he had been years before. His yellow cat eyes revealed themselves, glinting through the darkness as that wide, toothy grin reappeared.

The nightlight…

My first thought turned to the small, flickering bulb that had been plugged into the socket in the corner of our room for years. But now it was with my daughter. Keeping her safe. Keeping him away from her. Taking my invitation to return after so long instead. To taunt me as he had so long ago. When I was her age.

The thick smell of sulfur clung to my nostrils again as I tried to turn to my wife. Tried to wake her. But I couldn't move. My body had frozen in place – still. In shock. Not even a scream could rise up from my lungs. Break free from my throat. I was paralyzed. Trapped. Stuck staring into the smoldering eyes of that man. The Watcher.

The one I'd managed to evade for so long. But once more, he'd found me. Found me through my daughter. A hereditary haunting.

I saw those slender arms extend from his sides – skeletal fingers long and outstretched. I tried to avert my eyes, to gaze at anything else I possibly could in the room, but I was met only with darkness. A darkness deeper than any other. The void of that man. That *monster*.

With all the force he could, he pressed his hands against my throat. Shoving downward. Pushing me deep into the mattress. I could feel his inky fingers singe against my neck. Tightening. Cutting off my air. But there was nothing I could do. I couldn't move. Couldn't scream.

And worst of all, I couldn't wake up. My mother had been wrong all those years ago. It wasn't a dream. Just a never-ending waking nightmare. One I was bound to for life. One that would follow me generation through generation.

One that would watch me even beyond the grave.

BLS

The Field

Published in Aphotic Realm (2020)

When I was young, I remember the field across the street. It stretched for what seemed like miles, ending at the foot of a dense forest that lead to the other end of town. As a child, I spent countless hours there with the other neighborhood kids. Our afternoons were spent in the tall grass, hiding in weeds and laughing until the sun began to set just beyond the trees. Though we always insisted to stay out past dark, our parents were adamant about coming home when the last light of day bid farewell. Before the shadows engulfed the land.

There were no streetlights in our neighborhood. We were in a quiet part of town, set back from the rest of the busy activities. Aside from the field, most of our streets were surrounded by the woods. And so, the people enjoyed their comfort of the dark. And the beauty of the moonlight and stars.

I remember the summer nights, watching the colors of sunset paint the skies, running through the grass. But only to the edge of the trees. The one thing we always knew better of, was than to enter the forest. My mother warned of its lack of trails and the wild animals that made it their home. We knew well of the coywolves that made their way out of the fields at twilight, prowling, until they slunk away in the morning dew and mist.

At night, from my bedroom that overlooked the field, I could hear their howls. Haunting. My mother always told me they'd sing after they caught their prey. Celebrating their kill in the moonlight. I knew the fields were full of deer once the sun set. And I'd seen my fair share of their skulls left behind—bones scattered. I'd nestle into my bed, trying to drown the coywolves out, waiting for dawn.

I spent every day in that field. Dragging my bike through the tall grass, following my friends as we made our oaths of staying friends forever. Oaths that vanished the same way we had, when we reached adulthood. None of us stayed in that town—except our parents.

When I visit these days, the neighborhood never really feels the same. But, it wasn't just the nostalgia that made my old home so unfamiliar to me. It was the streetlamps lining the length of the street—bulbs glowing the moment the sun began to dip behind those trees at the end of the…

What used to be the field we grew up in was now a complex. The tall grass mowed down and replaced with pavement. The rolling grass and what felt like endless land was now gone. Buried beneath civilization. Even the forest seemed to be pushed farther into the horizon. Trees removed so more homes could be built.

"They plan on cutting the whole wooded area back there down," my mother said. "The complex on the other side of town? They want to connect it with here. Making this all one, big, built up town."

While I'd moved to a busier nearby city with less trees and open fields, that was the one thing I wanted to come back. The feeling of nature. Of quiet. Not development.

"What about the wildlife?" I asked. "The deer? The coywolves…?"

My mother looked sorrowful. "Some were unfortunately destroyed. Paid hunters. The rest, well… They'll have to relocate. Find food somewhere else."

I stay in my old bedroom whenever I visit. The streetlights remind me too much of my own home, and I find myself drawing the curtains shut to drown them out. Even though the neighborhood definitely had been built up, it at least was quiet. I find it easy to fall asleep, to the silence of the old home. No sirens. No honking cars. No shouting. Just the stillness of the walls I was once familiar with. But, sometimes in the night, I would be awoken. Unsure by what, or why. But my first thought always is of the field.

Now, my mother has asked me numerous times during my stays if I could hear the coywolves at night. I tell her I'm always in such a deep sleep, that I hear nothing.

"It's quiet," I'd say.

She says her dog doesn't sleep at night. That he whines and paces and that she swears she can hear the howls of coywolves out in the field. I remind her that the field is gone. That, either they're out in the remainder of the woods, or, she's remembering phantom sounds from years before. She'd agree with me, though with a bit of uncertainty in her voice. But, I assured her, I'd only hear silence.

It's been a few months since I've stayed at my parents' home, but I've heard rumors. Reports of animals that had gone missing in the neighborhood. Rabbits, cats, small dogs. I'd remembered hearing stories from my mother about families down the street losing their cat. Missing signs posted up and down the length of the road. And then, how the neighbor's toy poodle disappeared. No sign of it digging its way out underneath the fence.

My mother began keeping her dog in at night. She claimed people were worried there were petnappers waiting in cars on the street. Picking up small animals for bait in dog fighting rings. While I understood her concern about keeping the dog in, I assured her that it was highly unlikely.

"There are streetlamps everywhere. You'd clearly see them."

A few more calls from my mother would come in, more stories of people's precious pets disappearing in the night. But, it was only when the reports began reaching newspapers that I showed concern.

Missing children.

Sunset had always been our curfew. Back then, though, there were no streetlights, so when night fell, it fell hard. Dark. These days, my mother says the children play out late. The lamps serve as extra light, and now, with the complex built up, there was nowhere for them to get lost. Nowhere for them, as she put it, to "trip and fall in some rut out in that tall grass."

"What about the forest?" I'd ask her. "You think they play out there?"

"Any sensible parent wouldn't let them."

I wanted to tell her how much times had changed from when I was growing up. Parents just weren't the same as they used to be. Less concern for their kids, let's face it. Technology had ways of making us mindless. Too wrapped up in other things.

I thought nothing more about it, even as more reports cropped up, until I stayed at my parents' while they were away, looking after their dog. The dying summer air made it cool at night, and crickets chirped out in development across the street. Longing, I'm certain, for the tall grass that used to cover the land. I stayed up late, sipping tea and reading a book. The glow from the streetlamps painted the room in eerie white. Almost the way the moon would when it peaked its harvest.

At first, I thought it was in my head. But, sometime around midnight, I heard a low howl from out beyond the houses. I took it to be the wind, and brushed it off, turning the page of my book. Downstairs, I could hear the dog whimpering. I hollered down and hushed him. It was far too late for him to go out.

It was quiet for a bit, but then, I heard it again. Louder. This time, a chorus of more than one. *Coywolves*. That, I couldn't be mistaken. Their howls echoed across the blacktop, through my window, and around my room. And they seemed endless. Haunting, like I remembered them as a child.

Peering out into the dim lit streets, I saw one. Silhouetted in the fog that rolled in from the forest. Standing there, at the edge of the drive into the complex. And then, just as quickly as I spotted it, it was gone. Like an apparition. Lost to the mist.

I heard from my mother they found children's clothes out in the woods when they were working on lodging. She says the police suspect wild animals, that the kids went off playing in the forest after dark. But, I'm not sure it was the children who stepped outside of their territory.

More trees have been cut down since I last heard from my mother. More houses set to be built. The deer have all left, the last stragglers hunted. And the missing animal reports don't stop.

But, what do you do when your home has been destroyed? You either leave—leave like we all did in adulthood—or stay behind and cling to that nostalgia. Deep under that concrete and blacktop, after all, there is a field. A field that has been there far longer than any of us have.

And in the night, celebrating, there are still voices of the coywolves.

Annie

Published in Twist & Twain Magazine (2020)

I'll never forget the Halloween I moved to Westport. It was a rough year for me – just barely 12 – moving in the hottest summer months to a new town in the middle of nowhere. Coming from the big city, the endless fields and forests were definitely new territory. Concrete was replaced with dirt and grass; skyscrapers, tall oaks. My mother assured me that I would adjust in time. That I'd feel more comfortable once I started school and made new friends. But, as the crisp September air set on the small town, I began to feel lonelier than ever. It was hard, being the new kid. And by the end of my first month of school, I had not one friend. Well… except for Annie.

I'd met her one day in the park after school, swinging on the swing set just beneath the old maple trees. Her auburn hair glistened in the afternoon sun, radiant like the freshly fallen autumn leaves. I still remember her smile, her deep cinnamon brown eyes and freckled cheeks. I remember her humming, kicking her legs higher and higher, lifting her into the air. I was hesitant to take the swing beside her, at first. And, quite honestly, was surprised when she acknowledged me when I did.

"Hi," she smiled. "My name's Annie… what's yours?"

I glanced over to her. "Ollie…"

"Hi, Ollie." There was a little laugh in her voice. "I haven't seen you around the park before. This your first time here?"

I nodded. "Yeah. My mom and I moved here last month. I'm… still getting used to everything."

Annie stopped swinging, dragging her feet through the dirt beneath the swing to come to a full stop. She looked over at me, smile never fading.

"Well, if there's anything you want to know, I got you." She winked. "I've been here my whole life. I know lots of the places around for playing games and stuff. I can show you some time!"

I felt a smile tugging at the corners of my mouth. This was the first time anyone had voluntarily offered to do anything with me in this town. And, I thought, getting to know some of the best places to hang out would be a plus.

"That would be great," I said.

We talked for a while longer, Annie asking questions about where I moved here from, what the city was like… all the basic new kid questions. I asked her a little about herself, as well. Where she lived, about her parents, what grade she was in.

"I just live with my dad," she said, quietly. "And… I don't go to school. Not anymore, anyway."

"Really?" I asked, surprised. "How come?"

Annie was about to answer me, when I heard my mother calling from the park bench. It was getting late in the evening, and I knew she wanted to be home to make dinner. I smiled one last time at Annie, extending my hand in friendship. She took it, eagerly, and smiled back. It was only then that I noticed the bruises just beneath her shirt sleeve. I thought nothing of it – what child would – and said goodbye.

For the first night in what felt like forever, I was eager to tell my mother about my day. And my new friend, Annie.

For the next few weeks, Annie and I played together every day. I would find her on the swing at the park, humming, and waiting for me. And then, we would explore the small town, heading up and down old streets and between shops. Annie had a story about everything.

"My dad says it gets real busy through here this time of year. Something about 'peepers' coming through," she said.

"Peepers?" I asked.

She made her eyes wide, making faux binoculars with her hands around them. "Yeah, peepers. I guess people from the city that come up here to look at the leaves changing or something." She looked at me. "I guess that makes you a peeper, Ollie."

While we spent our time hanging around the storefronts and at the park, our favorite place to go ended up being just at the edge of town. To a wooded area, what must have been hundreds of acres. We never went too deep into the forest, Annie warned me that there were wild animals there: bears, coyotes, and rumored cougars.

"I wouldn't doubt it if the boogieman lived out here, too!" she'd say. "Probably out in a little shack by the creek."

We'd sit out in the foliage, looking up at the gray skies hidden behind the bare branches of trees. Just talking. Laughing. Living childhood the way we all should. Free.

As it became closer to the end of October, however, I started noticing that the bruises on Annie's arms were thicker. Darker. I didn't want to ask about them at first—most kids had bruises. Even *I* had my fair share from falling off my bike or off of swings. But, there was something about Annie's that didn't seem right.

"What… what happened to your arm?" I asked, once I had the courage to do so.

I could tell I'd hit a nerve. Annie's bright smile quickly faded, and she tugged her sleeve down to cover the dark marks.

"O-oh… it's nothing…"

I didn't question her further. Instead, we just laid together in silence, on our backs, atop a carpet of dead leaves. We watched the autumn gray turn above us, brushed by the skeletal branches—the first sign that winter would soon be on its way. After a long while, Annie finally spoke again.

"Sometimes, I wish I could move away."

I looked over at her. "M-move away?"

"Yeah," she said, feigning a soft smile. "Somewhere far away. Somewhere new. Where no one knows me. Where I can… just start over."

I was silent. She rolled over onto her side, facing me.

"You're lucky, Ollie. You're free."

Looking back, I liked to believe that Annie got her wish. Her dream of moving away to some unknown place, new and fresh. We had been looking forward to Halloween all month, and were so excited to show each other our costumes. I went as a vampire – thinking it would be cool to get to use the fake blood capsules in my mouth. I'd seen the teenagers use them, and convinced my mother I was finally old enough myself to give them a try. And Annie... Annie went as an angel. Her white dress reflected the dim streetlights, making her stand out brilliantly against the shadows. I'll never forget how she looked that night. Shining. Radiant.

It still gets to me that, that Halloween night was the last time I ever saw her.

I remember getting candy, laughing as we filled our pumpkin buckets. We rang doorbells, scrunching our noses at every raisin and popcorn ball tossed our way – and playfully arguing over which candy was the best.

"Well, I'll trade three of my Three Musketeers for one of your Twix," I'd said.

"No way!" Annie shot back.

When we were done in our neighborhood, we wandered to the edge of the wooded area where we played daily. Annie was quiet, gazing out at the trees. The darkness. I approached her, speaking softly.

"Annie..."

She didn't look at me. She was still for a moment longer before responding, low and distant.

"I should get home... My dad won't want me out this late."

I never truly got to say goodbye. Annie turned from the forest, from *me*, so quickly – and went back home. The next day, I didn't see her at the park where we usually would meet. I sat on the swing for hours, clutching my bucket of Halloween candy, waiting for the trades we had promised. But she never showed.

Rumors began to spread through my school of kids who had known Annie, saying that she probably ran away. She'd spoken of it often. Ever since her father pulled her out of school. But I didn't understand. I knew how much she longed to escape this town and the confines it left us in. But, I never thought she would just up and leave in the night. Without a word. A *goodbye*. At least, not to me.

I never stopped thinking about Annie, not even after my teen years. Adulthood. There always had been a feeling of loss when the leaves began to change and the air grew cool and crisp. And every Halloween, I've always wondered about her. About where she went. Why she hadn't said goodbye. And, ultimately, if she found her freedom. Her happiness. And, if she ever thought of me.

This Halloween, I finally felt the excitement I had when I was a child. My son, Devin, was finally at the age where he could enjoy the day. In previous years, my wife and I always brought him around to a few of the local houses, but he was too young to really understand, or eat the candy. Now that he was 5, he definitely had more of the Halloween spirit in him. He chose his own costume this year – a dinosaur onesie – and had been more than excited about going around to get candy.

When the sun began to sink behind the hills, we headed out, flashlights in hand. Devin walked close beside me, his little pumpkin candy collector swaying at his side. We hit up the first few houses on our side of the street, making our way to the end of town, just beyond the storefronts. Devin was much livelier this year and into the whole Trick-or-Treating thing, and so, going the extra distance wasn't as difficult as it had been in past years. A cranky toddler definitely didn't stand well for being that far from home late at night.

As we made our way towards the end of the street, I could have sworn I heard a soft humming coming from behind me. I glanced back, expecting to find a trailing child, on their way for their last rounds before curfew set in; but, all I was met with was darkness. The distant streetlamps burning in the center of town. I was still for a moment, keeping a firm grip on Devin's hand, before I heard him begin to hum. That same tune I thought came from behind me.

"Dev'…," I said softly. "You… you heard that, too?"

My son looked up at me and nodded. Again, I thought I heard that same, cheery, but at the same time, somber, humming. Only this time, it was coming from the trees. The wooded area just before us. I went to head back towards the center of town, back to the other houses on the opposite side of the street, leading home, when my cellphone rang. It was my wife, late at work due to overtime. I answered, focusing on the conversation and what I could around me.

"Hello?" I said. "Hey, honey… What? Another hour? They *know* you have a kid who you want to spend Halloween with. Couldn't they find someone else tonight?"

Somewhere, too focused in our call, I lost track of time. Lost track of everything outside the conversation. Devin managed to slip his hand from mine, making his way towards the forest. I heard him humming, softly, in the background of my call, but failed to realize that he had stepped away. Stepped to the edge of the wood. Only when I hung up did I realize him there, as if in a trance, staring off into the wall of trees.

"Devin?" I hurried over to him, taking his hand back. "Devin, what have I told you about wandering off? It's dark."

Devin was quiet. He ignored my question, answering only with, "But… the girl…"

I looked around, unsure of who he was talking about. I hadn't seen anyone near us—regardless of how little focus I had while on my call.

"What girl?" I asked.

Devin slowly raised his hand, pointing out into the darkness of the trees. Sure enough, there, deep between the branches and trunks, I could make out a figure in all white. And then, the humming. That humming I knew I had heard before. The tune my son began to mimic.

I felt Devin yank his hand away from me once more, this time hurrying into the trees, towards the figure. I called out to him, immediately following. The figure shifted, as if airy, floating away through the trees. But, Devin followed. I kept calling out to him, my heart pounding, flashlight frantically trying to light my path. It was only when we reached the edge of a rocky slope that caught up to my son, stopping beside him and scooping him into my arms.

"Don't *ever* run off again," I said sternly, trying to catch my breath—both from exhaustion and fear. "Do you understand me? What if something happened to you? What if you fell? Or got lost? Or—"

Devin wasn't paying any mind to me. He only continued to stare at the bottom of the slope. I slowly shone my flashlight down the leaf and rock ridden decline, the shaft of light catching on broken twigs and dead grass. Yet, just at the edge of where the light no longer could shine, it caught on something bright. White. Radiant.

I had to allow my eyes to adjust to the darkness, and the frail light my flashlight offered. But, what I saw, was no trick of shadow or light. It was a dress, once pure white, now tattered and torn by the elements – stained with dirt and mud and time. But, it wasn't the dress that brought the feeling of dread to the pit of my stomach.

Nor was it when my son, tightly gripping my shirt, in a sad tone, said, "Annie…"

It was what was in the dress. That once pure, white angel dress. There was nothing left but old bones, skin rotten and decayed, graying, pulled tight. The eye sockets were hollowed out, every ounce of flesh shriveled or picked clean by the forest. Picked clean by time itself. And the blood. The dried blood, now browned and thick, that coated the neckline of the dress – staining down the chest. The only feature that hadn't been warped, tainted, was the auburn hair that still clung to the thin scalp attached to the skull.

I felt sick. But, yet, I couldn't remove the ray of light from the corpse. The corpse of the child, buried partly by old, decaying leaves. And by the town itself.

The next morning, the police took to the woods, excavating the body from deep within the trees. It was identified as Annie, the young girl I had befriended all those years ago. The one I last saw in that white angel dress, late one Halloween. They say she was murdered and discarded out there over the ravines – near the creek. Where no one hardly ever traveled. No one except us, when we were kids.

They suspected it was her father. The drunken old man who had pulled her from classes to "homeschool" her, when the worry of check-ins became too heavy. Too risky. When the bruises on her arms began to show. She dreamed of running away. Away from the town. Away from her *father*. The only real boogieman that ever existed.

When they finally closed the case and laid her to rest, I stayed beside the grave. Lost, and looking for words. But the only ones I was able to find in that cold, autumn gray, were the ones I longed to have said all those years before.

"Goodbye, Annie…"

Every Halloween, I still wait at the edge of the wood, like I did the night I last saw her. I wait for just before curfew, when the streets become quiet, and the last of the children head home to count their candy and turn in to sleep. Only then will I hum that song that was once familiar to my ears. The one from the park swing, so long ago. And I wait. And wait. Until the echo rises from beyond the trees. Soft. Sweet. Often accompanied with the cool breeze, wrapping its way around my being.

I'm lucky, Ollie. I'm free.

MARK
'21

BLS

In Autumn (Ghosts)

Published in Page & Spine Magazine (2020)

I still look for you in autumn;
in the cool breath of dying summer,
lining goosebumps on my flesh—

like dewdrops.

I search the amber haze,
the slanted October light;
longing for ghosts and apparitions—
pale memories in the fog.

I wait for the mist of my lover.

Beneath bare branches,
hollowed holes in the oak,
I listen for a voice—
an airy echo.

But sleepy silence is all returned,
the brisk chill gnawing at the throat—
suffocating—
in the bitter twilight.

Alone I stand on the path we met.

Breathing in the stale husks of harvest,
an early winter's grave;
I am left withered and broken—
abandoned—
decaying leaves on the doorstep of death.

The Devil's in the Details

Published in The Storyteller Series (2020)

Halloween had always been my favorite holiday. Every year when the leaves started to change and the air became cool and crisp, that sense of nostalgia would roll in. I remember those dark nights of my childhood, meeting up with friends in their busy neighborhoods and Trick-or-Treating. Laughing under street lights and trading candy. It was only when the local cops made their rounds, ushering us all home that we'd leave. The blanket of curfew in our town was always so strict. And, looking back as an adult, it seems to have gotten even earlier than my days.

As the years went on, I spent my time celebrating Halloween with classmates in college at rundown pizza joints in the city. The magic of my small hometown was lost amongst the city lights. There never seemed to be a curfew. And, quite frankly, there never seemed to be children. They'd all take to the wealthy, upper-crust neighborhoods on the east side.

The nights usually ended with a movie – John Carpenter's *Halloween*, the classic. Watched only in the glow of the orange fairy lights strung around my dorm. Jack o' Lanterns were forbidden on campus – the whole, "catching fire" thing. It just never felt the same as I remembered growing up. And I began to wonder if I'd outgrown the holiday… much like I felt I had Christmas.

It wasn't until I graduated with my Bachelor's and returned home the following summer that I began to feel that spark again.

Coming back to a small town after spending four years in the heart of the city was definitely culture shock. I'd forgotten how mundane life was. Everything had a schedule, everything was planned, and everything closed by 9pm. My college mindset still kept me up all hours of the night, drinking coffee and watching the sunrise. Only this time, they were over the distant mountains, not the parks and penthouses.

Yet, out of all the changes I had to adjust to, the one I just couldn't accept, was that my creative motivation was draining. Since a young age, I'd always been a writer. The love for the craft began as early as Kindergarten, when every Friday, my teacher would have us write short stories on index cards that she'd laminate and staple together into "books". We'd share our stories during snack time. The feeling of holding that little "book" in my hand – a finished product of my creation – kept me inspired. And so, I never gave up.

Majoring in Fiction Writing at one of the top universities for the craft in the country, I'd gotten so much feedback in my seminars and workshops. We were *always* writing. Always creating. But now, with no one to share my work with and critique, I felt that motivation diminishing. And for the first time in over four years, not one piece of mine was queried out to magazines or journals that summer.

I was convinced the small town took away that magic the same way the big city took Halloween.

It was nearing the end of July when I saw the ad in the paper that one of the bookstores would be hosting a Q&A event with a local author. I'd seen him around social media over the years. He went to my high school, briefly, and was the sort of guy who added everyone who was in the town (and neighboring towns) just to rack up his follower and like count. Personally, I'd never met him, but I figured this would be the perfect opportunity to experience what I had in college that I'd loved so much. And, just maybe, pitch an idea.

The night of his Q&A was dreary. Rain fell hard throughout the day and into evening. And the municipal parking lots were so far away. I was soaked by the time I made it in the doorway. The bookstore was on the corner of Main Street, bold on the outside, but tucked away on the inside. Everything was so dim – and the pouring rain offered no late evening light. The front of the store was all books. Most of them old and tattered. Had it not been for the coffee counter in the back, I was certain the smell of mildew would have been overpowering.

To what was my surprise, however, was how empty the shop had been. The only ones there aside from me were the barista and… the author. He was seated in the center of the shop on one of their lounge couches, sipping coffee and staring at us with a smile. I made my way over slowly, about to say something, but the author spoke first.

"Noah, right?"

He ushered me to take a seat on the couch across from him. I'll admit, I was taken aback by the fact he knew my name. I hadn't been in this town in at least four years – let alone never met the guy.

"Uh, yeah…" I responded. "How did—"

"Facebook." He took another sip of coffee. "We've interacted a few times on there. Usually on my writing posts."

"Oh, yeah. That's right." I chuckled lightly.

He extended his hand to me. "Jake Bechtold. But I'm sure you already knew that."

I smiled and accepted his shake. "Of course."

For the first time having met him in person, I got a good look at Jake. While he was only my age, he was already showing signs of balding – hair thinned out and receding. He almost resembled my father in that matter. He was also short in stature and certainly on the heavier side. But, the one feature I just couldn't get out of my mind were his eyes. The right was clouded over, almost nonexistent in its milky glaze. And the left just never looked forward. I found myself staring, and quickly averted my gaze, clearing my throat.

"So your book… Traditional? Or did you go the self-publishing or print-on-demand route?"

Jake grinned. "All traditional. I'd thought about self-publishing… more control, you know? But then I thought about all the marketing and money you gotta put into it, and… Nah. Just wasn't for me."

I was impressed. While I'd had my fair share of fiction published in literary magazines and journals, I'd yet to query anything of novel length work. The closest I'd ever gotten was a novella I'd knocked out during National Novel Writing month my first year of college. And that, I printed off some copies for family with a print-on-demand press. Nothing major.

"Wow. That's… that's amazing, Jake. Most people our age barely *complete* their novel projects, let along get one picked up by a publisher. Who's your agent?"

Jake laughed. "Agent? I'm my own agent, as far as I'm concerned. I wasn't going to waste my time querying out and waiting for representation. I had faith you know." He tapped the cover of the book resting on the table between us. "Sometimes, you just gotta live dangerously. Bite the bullet."

I stared down at the cover. "May I?"

"That's why you're here, isn't it?"

I took the book into my hands, the title, *Silent Winter,* staring back at me. I gently brushed my fingertips against the dust jacket. It definitely was a professional job – and the logo on the spine told me right away it was through an imprint of one of the Big Five publishing houses. Nearly *impossible* to acquire a deal with without an agent. I fingered through the cream pages, getting a feel of their thick texture. I only glanced up and back to Jake when he spoke again.

"You're a writer, too, aren't you?"

"Yeah." I found a weak laugh. "Just got my BA in Fiction Writing, actually."

"You're published, too, right?"

"I mean, some smaller stuff in magazines, yeah. Nothing major like a *novel.* At least, not yet anyway."

Jake smiled. "You're working on one though, right? What was it called again… *White Memory*?"

"Working title, yes. But…"

Again, I wasn't certain how he had known all of this. He said we'd followed each other on Facebook and we'd conversed a few times. But, I rarely spoke on my novel and my own writing. If anything, it was a status here or there when one of my short stories released. Just a link to the e-book as a failed attempt to plug my work.

"You don't have anything to worry about. You've got experience, credentials…" Though I knew he wasn't physically able to, I knew he was looking at me. "You're like me. You have desire. And when you want something that bad, you'll get it."

I stayed with Jake, talking writing and drinking coffee, until the shop closed just before 9pm. The awkwardness of the night vanished quickly once we got on the topic of our stories, my experiences in college, and the publishing process. Overall, Jake was a down-to-earth guy. And so, I brought up my offer, *pitch*, if you will, about looking to form a writing group in the town.

"I think it would be great, you know? Bringing together like-minded people who want to share their work and grow. Hey! If they're interested in publishing, we can go about teaching the ropes of that, too. You with the novels and me with the short prose."

Jake loved the idea. He confessed that he'd had similar ideas for months, but never had anyone who was interested in co-running it with him. No, he said no one who was *experienced* enough to run it with him. He said he knew a lot of teenagers in the town who would love to take it on, and a few others our age.

"We'll talk," was the last he said on the matter as we stepped outside into the gray.

I pulled the collar of my jacket up higher as Jake lit a cigarette. Just as we were about to head our separate ways, I stopped, digging in my pocket for my wallet.

"Oh! I almost forgot. *Silent Winter*? I want to get a copy."

Jake shook his head. "Don't pay me. Here." He extended the copy he had with him. "Consider it a gift. Writer to writer."

I didn't question him, not knowing what to say. I just took the book in surprise. "Thank you…"

As he crushed his cigarette butt into one of the puddles, he nodded his head to me in farewell and began to make his way to the crosswalk. Tucking his book under my jacket so it wouldn't get wet in the rain, I called out one last time.

"Jake! You never *did* tell me how you landed that book deal."

He turned his head back to me, and I could see his wide smile reflecting in the car lights. "Like I said, if you want something that bad, you'll get it. Sometimes, it costs you. Other times, well… there are things in this world we just can't explain."

Jake kept his promise about founding a writing program with me on Friday nights. We started off small, but as summer faded into autumn, we found our numbers were rising. Teens and young adults not only from our town got wind of our group, but from neighboring towns, as well. At first, we met in the bookshop, reading our stories and poems under the dim lights, devouring more caffeine than we ever could need. But once we outgrew the store, we moved to the library. And from there, Jake's place.

He lived in a rundown apartment just at the edge of the village. Just like most of the rest of town, there was no parking nearby, so everything was a trek. His apartment was on the first floor, and shared a large wrap-around porch with his neighbor upstairs. Most of the time, she was on the porch, rocking in her chair, talking to dead air.

"The kids all think she's a witch," Jake would say. "She's actually quite harmless. Sweet, if you get to know her."

For the few months we had been together, we all worked on small pieces from prompts and brought in our work-in-progress chapters and stories for critique. It was when October finally came that Jake proposed the idea of a scary story contest. The first contest that we'd be running as a group.

"Here's the deal. You all have 30 days to write your piece. It can be a poem, it can be a story… whatever. Just make sure it's the scariest thing you can think of."

The group, of course, became all chatter. Everyone was excited about testing the waters with a chilling tale – dark fiction, uncanny, true horror.

"We'll all meet on Halloween, here. Have a little party, you know? Noah and I will read all the pieces, by candlelight. At the end of the night, we vote for the scariest one. Deal?"

"And what do we get if we win?" one of the members, Tim, always questioning everything, asked.

I could see that smile on Jake's face again. The one I'd seen the day we first met, when I asked him about his book deal.

"A ribbon, a certificate, praise in our group," he said. "And, my publisher agreed to look at one of your manuscripts."

I could care less about the ribbon and certificate. I'd earned enough of those growing up and playing sports and winning local writing competitions and art shows. The thought of Jake's publisher, one of the Big Five, looking at *my* work? It wasn't imaginable.

And so, I spent the rest of the month penning the end of my manuscript, and working on what I thought to be the scariest story I could put together. But, I kept reminding myself, scary was more than just over the top monsters or gore. Yeah, those things were scary… but true fear came after the story was finished. The sense of everything being normal and fine, but, something off. Just slightly. The uncanny. The unknown. That's what *true* fear was. The things we couldn't quite explain.

I stayed up late into the early hours of morning, drafting my piece over and over again, polishing it. And then, on the morning on Halloween, I printed it. Nameless. Ready to be read by candlelight.

I spent most of the day on Halloween anxious. I just wanted, more than anything, to have my story win. To have the opportunity to bypass any agent queries, any representation. To just be able to stick my manuscript on the desk of the acquiring editors and hope for a miracle.

My friend Angela, who I'd been close with since middle school, kept assuring me that my piece was probably near perfect, and that the only real threat I had was Jake. Angela had been the first one to join the group, when I was desperately looking for members upon its announcement, and I knew she was a strong writer. We had spent most of our days in high school passing off our pieces in the hallways, reading and critiquing each other. And while I knew I had grown from years of refinement in my college courses, she surely had, as well.

It wasn't Jake I was worried about. It was her.

We spent the late afternoon getting our costumes ready, helping each other with makeup and being sure that everything fit just right. Angela insisted that we go together as a themed costume – Little Red and the Big Bad Wolf. She braided her hair overnight so that it fell in wavy curls for the party, keeping her hood down to show them off. And, just like her purse was usually overflowing with useful nonsense, so was her picnic basket. She packed cookies, candy, our printed stories, and a lighter—just in case Jake's candles wouldn't light with matches. As for my costume, my mother had stayed up late sewing faux fur into an old flannel shirt, giving off the authentic werewolf feel. She'd even taken the time to sew together and stuff a tail, and make furred gloves with claws. My mom always had the best made Halloween costumes over the years – and I couldn't wait to come home from the party to show her how well it looked on me.

Just as the sun began to set, Angela and I gathered our things and headed for Jake's apartment.

It wasn't until that night that I think I ever realized just how small the apartment was. With our whole group gathered on his couch, chairs, and the floor, it seemed even tinier between all the bowls of popcorn, chips, and candy. And the handful of opened pizza boxes and soda bottles.

"Do you get Trick or Treaters here at all?" Angela asked Jake once we were all settled.

"*Here*? Nah. This is just beyond the street lamps. Most parents take their kids into the village itself for Trick or Treating. There's a lot more going on. More light. Over here, we're pretty much forgotten," he said, then motioned to me. "Noah, how about we get those candles ready?"

Angela gathered all the printed out and handwritten stories and poems from the group while Jake and I went to the kitchen. By now, I'd removed my gloves and my wolf head mask so that I could properly see, and safely use the matchbook. Jake handed me a candle before striking a match and lighting his own.

"You nervous?" he asked.

"Nervous? What for?"

"For winning," he said, surely looking at me.

"I mean, yeah, aren't we all?" I said. "Everyone gets a little antsy when it comes to something like a prize being on the line. But at the end of the day, it's just about having fun."

"But is it really?"

I glanced over to Jake, his now-lit candle flickering in the dim kitchen light. I was without words, caught up in the dancing flame and how it barely reflected in his milky right eye. There was definitely a reflection there, but it seemed so distant. Lost in that white void.

"You're like me, Noah. You want something bad enough, you get it in the end. I've told you this. Sometimes, you gotta pay for it. Other times—"

"I know," I said. "Other times, there are things in this world you can't explain."

" 'Atta boy." Jake offered the matchbook to me. "The question is, just how bad do you want it? And just what are you willing to pay?"

I struck the match, looking into the flame. It seemed so tranquil at first, but with each of my breaths, I could see it become violent at the end of the stick. I thought about how badly I wanted that opportunity. No. How badly I *needed* that opportunity. Jake was right. We were a lot alike. And if he was able to do it, a writer with no credentialed background, surely *I* could. Right?

All I could see through the flickering candlelight were his eyes. Twisted and disfigured. Vision likely hindered to the point I was unsure how well he'd be able to read the stories – in the light, let alone in muted darkness. But, I told myself, writers didn't need their eyes to see. They needed their hands. Their voices. Their minds. Words lived in the head, after all. The eyes had nothing to do with that.

As I went to light the candle, I felt something hot against my fingertip. At first, I ignored it, but only for a moment. The searing pain quickly snapped me away from my thoughts and I looked down at the match to realize the flame had spread down the stick. Right to my finger. I quickly lit my candle and blew the match out, handing it to Jake as the burning sensation overtook my hand.

"You alright?" he asked.

"Yeah… just burned myself is all," I said. "I guess I took too long."

Jake set his candle down and got me a cold, wet washcloth to hold against my wound, and a Band-Aid. I looked down at my already blistering and bloodied burn as I bandaged it, cursing myself for being so clumsy. My nerves pulsed under the bandage, mixed with the pain that still overtook my fingertip.

"You okay to still do this?" Jake asked as I held my candle closer.

"It's just a little burn," I said. "I've been ready for this all month."

The stories we wrote were all anonymous to the group. Only Jake and I knew who penned what – for the sake of awarding the prize at the end. I kept my stack of stories close, since beyond the flickering candlelight, there was nothing but darkness. I couldn't even make out the faces of the rest of the group, though I knew they were sitting right before me. It was so strange, how in the faint light, you could almost fall under a sort of trance. Nothing in the room seemed real, and my focus only became on the flame and the paper before me.

Jake and I took turns reading. The stories ranged from Creepypasta inspired killers to poems that seemed like old curses. A few had twists that came out of nowhere – thrown in for the sake of trying to give that eerie feeling, but failing miserably. Others, I felt just tried too hard. But it was when Jake read his story that I actually got a sense of competition. And that, perhaps, his writing was far better than I had anticipated.

"There are some things we can't explain in this world," he began, "and others, well, we have to pay a price…"

He read of a writer who was down on his luck, seeking his big break. He was young, determined, desperate. I just kept my gaze on my candle, listening to his story, taking in every word. The writer in his story kept facing rejection. Pieces passed up by agent after agent, until he just couldn't take it anymore. He wanted his work to be shared, to be heard, so badly. To the point he would do anything to achieve it. And so, he took matters into his own hands. He willed himself away, to a place between realms – between time itself. And there, he forged a deal with an entity, some dark spirit, for the deal of a lifetime. He got his book deal, he got a hefty advance, and the praise? Well, that just came naturally. The only price? His eyes.

"A writer doesn't need eyes, after all," Jake continued. "Words live in the heart, the mind, the soul. On lips."

The flame of my candle flickered dim and I breathed heavy.

"Besides, eyes aren't worth keeping when the shadows stare back at you."

There was nothing but silence in the room. I wasn't sure if the group was bored by Jake's story – if it went over their heads – or if they were taken back by true fear that they couldn't respond. Yet, from the corner of my eye, in the candlelight, I saw Jake turn to me. For the last story of the night. Mine.

I held the candle close, my hand trembling as I began. I didn't want to give away the anxiousness in my voice – spoiling the fact that this was, indeed, my story. After all, I wanted this. And blowing my cover wasn't an option.

I told the story of an estranged family, living out on an old farm far away from civilization. The children, newly adopted, spent their days in the fields, performing daily chores and learning the ways of life. It read very southern gothic – like something from the mind of Sam Shepard – nothing like I normally wrote. I carefully read my words, describing the fields and the dark shadows the roamed between the wheat, and the post at the far end of the property where no grass around it grew. I was waiting to instill that final bit of dread at the end, giving away that the family had been adopting out children from various orphanages over the years for work, and then, if they weren't what they had hoped for, disposing them in the mass grave out by the post. Not monsters. Not ghosts. Just the unnatural fear that something was slightly off. Slightly wrong. Enough to keep the mind stuck on those small elements, even long after the story had finished.

As I neared the end of the piece, I glanced up looking out into the sea of shadows before me. I knew I wouldn't be able to see the faces of the group, let alone their silhouettes. It was nearing 10pm now, and darkness had overtaken every corner and crevice of the apartment. But, yet, there was *one* figure that I *could* make out. Standing, against the back wall.

They were nothing more than silhouette, an endless black void amidst the shadows. From what I could see, they were wearing an overcoat and a wide brimmed hat. And, they just stood there. Unmoving. I glanced back down at my paper and continued reading, being sure to keep looking up every few words to see if the figure was still there. And he was. Silent.

My candle flickered again, and I reached the final paragraph of my story. My mind worked hard at trying to comprehend the figure, while still processing the words on the page. Why was this the only person I could see in the room? Was the candlelight somehow making the back wall lit just enough that I could see whoever was standing there, but not those sitting before me? No, I told myself, because then, why couldn't I see the lamp or the bookshelves silhouetted, as well? And it's dark. That was what kept coming back to the forefront of my mind. There was no way anyone could be seen in a room of shadows. They'd have to be darker than pitch. Black-on-black. A void. It just wasn't possible.

I looked back down at the paper in my hands, voice clearly quivering as I read the final sentence aloud. "But sometimes, I stay up late and think about them… the shadows, the ghosts, and the monster… and all that lays beneath that old, splinted post."

There was a symphony of clapping coming from before me, and it broke me away from staring at that figure against the wall. I mustered a smile as Jake flicked the light switch, flooding the apartment in light. Immediately, I returned my gaze to where it had been standing. But there was nothing there. Not even a *coatrack*. Just the bare and empty dirty wall.

I blew my candle out, tracing the faces and costumes of the group before me. No one was even wearing anything similar to what I had seen – had one of them chosen to stand during my piece. I shook it off after a moment, accepting that it most likely was from the lack of light and the fact we were sitting around in the dark reading scary stories. Surely, my mind had been wandering. Jake was the one to finally pull me back to reality, breaking my thoughts of shadows.

"So, it's time to vote. We're just going to do this by a raise of hands, and you can only vote *once*, so make it count."

"Can we vote for our own?" Tim asked, his hockey mask now pulled up and resting atop his head. "You know, so we have a better chance of winning?"

"Vote for whoever you want, so long as you just cast *one* vote," Jake replied, clearly annoyed with Tim's questioning.

I looked out at the group again, ready to count up the hands that would be raised for each story title. My heart was pounding again, riddled with the same anxiety I had earlier. And Angela had been right – Jake's story was the one that brought the most fear to me. He was, as much as I didn't want to admit it, an amazing writer.

"*Headless Hollow... Jack the Killer... Curse of Deadwood Lake...*"

Jake read the titles and I watched as only a few hands moved – Tim's immediately flying up for *Headless Hollow*, the only vote for his knock-off and cheaply written twist piece. It was only when Jake reached the final two titles that the hands began to show in numbers.

"*The Devil's in the Details...*"

That was Jake's piece. Those, *details* I'm sure being the contract the writer in the story had signed with the entity. Or, the publisher. There were quite a few hands raised, and I tallied them up – a landslide compared to the other titles. Now, it was only mine left.

"And finally, *Where the Grass Won't Grow.*"

It was a minor victory. Only by two hands – Angela, and a quiet girl, Kaylee, I'm certain. But somehow, I had managed to pull through and take the victory that night with the scariest story of the bunch. Angela took a picture of me holding up my ribbon and certificate, and we all got another handful of candy in before heading out for the night.

It was 11pm on the dot, and I wanted to catch my mother before she turned in to sleep. My costume, at least, I thought, looked great. And I wanted to show her how well it fit and looked on *me*. That, and, of course, I wanted to show her my finger. Where the flame had burned me still stung, and I wanted to make sure it wasn't more serious than I thought.

We all said our farewells, congratulating one another once again before going our separate ways. I thanked Angela for helping me get ready and told her I'd see her in the morning to plan for a shopping weekend. I was the last one on the porch, with Jake, and I couldn't help but smile at him.

"Not bad," he said, lighting one of his cigarettes. "I like what you did there. Not too over the top, you know? You took the more, horrors of real life and played with that. I guess that does make for a scarier story than something supernatural, you know?"

"Yeah, but the supernatural can be just as terrifying. Your story… well…"

Jake smirked. "Ah, that old thing? That was more for the kids of the group. You know they jump whenever anyone mentions a boogieman."

"That's true…"

Jake patted my shoulder. "You deserved it."

I nodded, not sure if I wholeheartedly agreed or not. But, I thanked him again for the party. I wasn't going to lie, it was probably the first Halloween I'd had since childhood where I got to dress up and hang out with a bunch of people over food and scary stories. Far better than the lonely nights in my dorm after coming back from the run-down pizza joint.

"We'll discuss the details about getting your manuscript to my editor over the weekend," he said. "If you don't want the offer, you don't have to take it up. You know that. But, if you do… well. Just sleep on it."

I chuckled. "You *know* I want it."

Jake stared back with a small smirk of his own. "Yes. I suppose you do."

He picked up the jack-o-lanterns he had lining the steps, blowing them out one by one. I headed back to my car, down the dark streets of town, eager to get home and not only show my mother my complete costume, but also to get some rest. It was, after all, a very long day.

I pulled into my driveway at 11:37pm – later than I had hoped, but I knew my mother would still be awake. She always stayed up until about midnight reading. And sometimes, even later if she knew my younger brother or I would be out. Yet, as soon as I stepped through the front door and into the living room, I was met with nothing but silence.

All the lights were out, casting deep shadows through the room and up the stairwell leading to my bedroom. I knew that even if my mother had turned in to bed, she *always* at least kept the light on for us. Maybe this time, I told myself, she forgot. Or the bulb burned out. But, even the silent stillness felt off. Normally, if I came home after everyone else had turned in for the night, the dog would start barking – aware that someone was in the house after bedtime. But tonight, there wasn't one peep. The only thing that my mind *did* register, however, was the faint flickering of the hall nightlight my mother had installed years before. It was mainly there to serve as extra lighting if someone had to get up and use the bathroom in the late night. So no one would trip over the dog's toys he carelessly left scattered. I stared at it, watching each of its feeble flashes in the dark hallway. How much it reminded me of the candle in my hand from earlier that night. Memorizing. Trance-like.

I headed upstairs to get changed for the rest of the night, but made sure to take a few pictures of my costume beforehand. I realized I never really got any. Angela and I had been too busy getting our stories together and the cookies she made packed before the party. I took a few selfies and posted them to Facebook, timestamped 11:45pm. The only other status that caught my eye as I was turning my phone off for the night was Jake's. Just a simple, "thank you to all who made this a great Halloween!" I liked it, and changed before turning in to bed.

Sleep that night was nearly impossible to find. I kept tossing and turning underneath the covers, caught up on the shadows that overtook the room. They were dark in the corners, endless. But, the set of shadows that I just couldn't keep my eyes off of were the ones by my closet – at the far end of the room. They'd gathered to form a figure. Tall. In an overcoat and wide brimmed hat. The same figure that was at Jake's apartment.

Was it my mind? I was sure that's all it was. It was late, and I'd been overthinking. There were too many scary stories floating around in my mind, and too much sugar still in my system. I closed my eyes, trying my hardest to find sleep, but it just wouldn't come. And so, again I found my mind wandering. Looking in corners. Only, this time, the figure seemed closer. Moving ever so slightly towards the foot of my bed.

Sleep on it.

I heard Jake's words in my head, thinking about the potential book deal. About forwarding my manuscript to his editor. About this opportunity that I know I'd most likely never get again. *Sleep on it.*

I couldn't just *sleep* on it. Not when I couldn't find sleep. I'd been wide awake, heart pounding against my chest from what I wasn't sure was fear or nerves. Excitement? I didn't know.

Do you want it?

Of course I did. I'd said it myself on Jake's porch. There was nothing I wanted more. I closed my eyes, attempting to find sleep one final time as the clock ticked away the hours into early morning. But, even when I would get comfortable, I still felt like something was watching. Keeping me from slumber.

I opened my eyes to see nothing but endless blackness before me. A void deeper than the shadows themselves. And that stench… It smelled of thick sulfur, emanating from the darkness. It was unbearable. Glancing up, I saw nothing but two dim flickers of what must have been eyes, staring down at me. Hidden deep within that void. Like frail candles, fighting the wind. I swallowed hard, shutting my eyes tightly before reopening them. Trying to will away the entity I knew was standing before my bed. A trick of the mind. A trick of the light, or, lack thereof. But it wouldn't leave. No matter how many times I opened my eyes and shut them, it was still standing there. Menacing. And that smile… Through the darkness, I knew I could see it. That wide, toothy grin.

Do you want it?

More than anything…

I awoke late the next morning, almost noon, after finally having been able to fall asleep. I wasn't sure when it was that I managed to finally drift off, but even with the rest, I still felt tired. Worn out from the night before. My mother was doing the dishes when I entered the kitchen groggily, and she couldn't help but laugh.

"Had a long night partying, huh?" she asked. "What time did you get home anyway? I waited up late for you."

"A little after 11:30," I said. "I thought you were going to be awake, but…"

My mother stopped her washing and looked at me. "11:30? You were *not* home at 11:30."

I was confused. Surely I had been. The clock at Jake's house said it was 11pm when we all decided to head home for the night—and the clock in my car was always accurate.

"We left Jake's at 11. I mean, I hung around to talk for a few, but I got here a little after 11:30… like I said."

"Noah," my mother's voice was stern and sincere. "I waited up until nearly 1am for you. The baseball game went into overtime – it must have ended around 12:30. Your father went to bed as soon as it was over, but I stayed up waiting. You never came home."

Had what my mother said been true, at the time I walked in, I would have found the living room shrouded in light. The television would have been on and blaring, my father getting worked up by his team's, most likely, eventual loss. My brother would have been asleep on the couch, dog beside him, and my mother reading. With the lamp beside the front door on. That light she *always* left on each and every night we were out late. The one that was off when I came home the night before. At 11:30pm.

"But I *did*!" I told her. "I even went upstairs and took photos… posted them to Facebook. Look, they have a time stamp."

I opened my phone and showed her the photo's stamp: October 31st, 11:43pm. It was clearly me, in my werewolf costume, taken in my bedroom. My mother said that, maybe my time on the phone was off and reflecting that, but then I showed her the post to Facebook. Twelve hours before.

"11:45," I told her. "You can't tell me Facebook's time is off, *too*."

My mother looked pale. I could tell that she was being honest about the game – probably even telling me to look up the final score and see for myself what time it ended. But, how could it have been that I walked into a quiet and dark house at the time she said was the height of the game. All light up.

"Everything was dark," I told her. "Everything… well… except the nightlight."

She looked concerned.

"The one in the hall. I came home and that was flickering… but that was it. The dog didn't even bark. I just figured you all went to bed."

"Noah…" My mother's voice was quiet. "That nightlight in the hall hasn't had a bulb in it in almost 3 months…"

She proceeded to show me the bulb-less light, and I felt a sick twisting in the pit of my stomach. We both were telling the truth, weren't we? I knew what time I'd come home…

"I left at 11pm," I said again. "I wanted to be home before you were asleep. To show you my costume. And, well…" I held up my finger, still wrapped in the Band-Aid. "I burned myself last night on one of the matches we were using to light the candles for our scary story contest. It was pretty bad. I wanted you to look at it."

I peeled the bandage off and held my hand out to her. My mother took it gently and looked, but more in question than concern.

"It must not have been *that* bad," she said. "I can't even see a mark."

I looked at my finger in disbelief, but, she was right. The blister and blood that was forming the night before, that burned unbearably, was gone. Skin repaired. Smooth. As if nothing had ever happened.

"I don't…" I began. And I couldn't finish.

I didn't know what to say at that point. Nothing made sense.

My mother tried to make light of the situation. "You weren't doing any rituals last night, were you?" She laughed. "Maybe you got stuck in a time warp or something… another dimension."

A place between realms – between time itself.

"Oh, that reminds me. Jake called early this morning," my mother said.

"Jake…?"

"He said something about one of your stories and an editor? Did you get something published again?"

"Uh, well, not yet," I said. "I think he was working to see if my manuscript could get picked up by his publisher… if, I wanted to accept the offer."

My mother looked thrilled. "Really? That's amazing, honey! I know how much you've been wanting to get your longer works out there. Fingers crossed, okay?"

I didn't say anything in response. I headed back to my bedroom and called Jake.

"Hey, Noah! Yeah, my editor read your manuscript – at least the partial – and she loved it. Says it's definitely a fresh new voice they would love to share. She wants to know when you're free to chat, you know, go over all the details."

"Jake…" I was quiet. "How did she get my manuscript? I've been asleep, I haven't—"

"You said yourself last night that it's all you've wanted. I mean, I know I told you to sleep on it, but… you sounded so sure. I had your file saved, you know, back when you sent it to me earlier this month for my opinion? I just sent it over myself, to get the ball rolling. And, hey, they *loved* it!"

I was quiet. This news should have been exciting. A dream come true. But for some reason, it instilled fear in me. That fear of something unexplainable.

"I just gotta know, so I can get back with her… if you accept," Jake said. "Is this something you want?"

Silence. Deep in thought.

"Yes…," I said softly, but certain. "More than anything."

The contract was simple, just the standard stuff. And the advance was decent – a good $15k before royalties. It was just a quick discussion and meeting with the editor, a simple sign off on paperwork.

"The devil's in the details," was all I remember her saying to me as she slid my contract across the desk to me.

I owed so much to Jake for his help in getting my career off the ground, but, I'd noticed that after my book had launched and hit shelves, I barely saw him anymore.

"Sorry, Noah. I'm busy… you know how the writer life is. Always gotta work on something fresh and new."

With his lack of participation, our group slowly dismantled, too. Teenagers graduating and moving away to college, others losing interest in writing altogether.

And so, my Q&A, much like his, was spent alone – on a dreary and rainy evening in the mid-summer. But, even with the lack of support from the locals, just being able to hold that finished product in my hand – that beautiful dust jacket with *White Memory* displayed proudly across the cover was enough. I had done it. I'd *finally* done it.

I still stayed up late into the early hours of morning, drinking coffee and writing. New stories this time, ones not so light. Not so kind. I've become convinced that the shadows have persuaded me otherwise. To tell their stories, of the deep dark. The uncertain. The unknown.

And the sleep never comes. On the off days that I try and catch up on my rest, I still feel those flickering embers of eyes burning from the corner of my room. The corner where the darkness collects into endless voids. Haunting. It never stops watching and it never leaves me be. I'd tried so many home remedies to attempt to sleep. Cutting back on the coffee, making sure I'm in bed at a decent hour, aroma therapy… But nothing seems to quell the inner dread in the pit of my stomach. The feeling that everything is normal, but yet, still slightly off. And I've run out of ideas. Both for the mind and for stories. The words just won't come anymore. I'm convinced, it's because the eyes have simply seen too much.

But, what would you be willing to pay? Is there any price too much when there's something that you want more than anything? Jake was right. He and I were alike. We were passionate. And we knew what we wanted, regardless of the cost. No matter how unexplainable it was to the rest of the world. After all, a writer is nothing without his words. They were as precious as air itself. They lived in the heart, the mind, the soul…

And without them, the darkness would just get thicker. Deeper.

I lit a candle on my desk, watching as the flame mimicked the burning eyes of the figure before me. Lost in that trance I had been that Halloween night. Surrounded by members of our old group. Desperate.

What would you be willing to pay?

Words were all I needed now. Off lips and tongues and fingers. Pages.

Besides, eyes aren't worth keeping when the shadows stare back at you.

Sunless Dawn

Published in School Lunch Zine (2020)

The world was still the day the sun didn't rise. Silence and darkness overtook the once bustling town, streets empty and abandoned. The radio signals had died down, distress calls from the evening prior fading out into the sunless dawn. Into the barren and desolate streets. Into the eternal night. But yet, the echoes of the emergency evacuation pleas still rang heavy through the thoughts of the townsfolk. Escape, or so they were told, was the only promise of freedom.

Zeke was among the first to venture out into the streets, his younger brother Clyde trailing closely at his side. The air was thick and cold, lingering in metallic staleness that had come with the migrating winds. Winds that had all but tattered the once lively town. The debris left behind from their gusts littered the roads, making it nearly impossible to travel safely. Zeke turned on his flashlight, shining it through the deep shadows, searching for any signs of life.

"Where is everyone?" Clyde asked softly, careful to not stray too far behind his older brother.

"Inside, I would assume," Zeke replied. "That or they've all evacuated. Hopefully before all the power died."

He shone his flashlight down the sidewalk, reaching buildings tightly closed up as if abandoned. Yet, only 24 hours prior, everything was in full operation. Children laughing, vehicles crowding the streets…

It was only when the first meteor had struck that the town fell into panic.

The impact was abrupt. No radar had tracked it falling out of its path, and certainly not plummeting to the land below. The sun was still high in the sky then, offering warmth as the ground trembled beneath the collision. There were screams – those nearby going to investigate once all had calmed down. To see what had happened.

The ground had split in two, a cavernous crater left behind where the meteor had sunk – deep into the crust. There were whispers, townsfolk wondering where it had come from. Why nothing had been tracked on radar. The broadcasts began then, reporting that there had been an incident. Instructing all to stay away from the impact site; lest the ground give in and take a few lives with it.

A few hours later, the next one struck. This one, smaller in size, but the damage far greater. It hit a home in the center of town, breaking through the roof and foundation, dragging it down beneath the surface. Now, the fear began to set in. The initial spark of wonder and amusement of the initial strike were gone. This meteor, as the radio broadcasts had stated, was too close for comfort. It was then that the town was advised to remain indoors. Should any more bits of space debris make their way to land.

And sure enough, they did. A hailstorm of tiny pebbles plummeted towards the town, cracking windows and battering streetlamps. The winds came with them, too – heavy. They howled and tore through the buildings and streets, sending the stones with them. They ricocheted off of parked vehicles, homes, and pavement. Bringing nothing but destruction in their path. But, it was the final meteor that truly devastated the town. Sending it into a realm of shadows and cold and silence.

The impact was enough to rattle the foundation of every building that remained standing. The force cracked the pavement and ground, spider webbing into sinkholes that dragged half of the residential homes under. The radio signals were lost – the final words and pleas of the emergency broadcast to evacuate. To find safety and shelter elsewhere. And in the fading of the voices through static and wire, the sun disappeared from sight.

The force had knocked the planet out of orbit. Away from the sun.

The air became colder as Zeke and Clyde made their way through the rubble, still searching for any sign of life. Haze clouded their vision, likely heavy from the dust that still settled from the crumbling buildings – lost to the depths of the ground beneath them.

"Maybe we should call out in case someone's there," Clyde whispered. "What if someone is hurt?"

Zeke didn't respond. He only continued to shine his flashlight through the darkness, making out shapes through the mist and shadows. From the corner of his eye, he thought he saw something move – shift – amongst the debris. The faint *clack* of stone upon stone echoed through the vacant street, and he shone the light towards the ruins of a collapsed department store. Swallowing hard, he gripped Clyde's hand, dragging him along behind him cautiously.

But, when they reached the pile, there was no trace of life. Only old cracked stone and rubble. And a body… Broken and twisted in a ghastly manner against the pavement. Crushed by the foundation. Clyde gasped and covered his eyes at the sight, his brother only managing a weak grimace.

"Come on…," he coaxed. "Let's get out of here."

The craters left behind by the meteors seemed bigger than the brothers remembered as they made their way towards the end of town. More splinters left behind in the crust, more buildings sinking to never-ending trenches and pits. And the bodies… So many had been left behind in the streets. At least, those that hadn't been swallowed up by the sinkholes. They all lay bruised and bloodied, many with craters of their own broken through the flesh down to the bone. Mangled. The boys tried to keep their focus ahead of them and not on the death that littered the streets. That filled the air in a thick and heavy odor. There had to be someone left. Someone who hadn't fled and made it through the destruction. They made it out, they kept telling themselves. Surely someone else had, too.

They continued on through the empty silence, following the old road that led in and out of the town, until Clyde stopped short. Zeke followed suit, turning to him, about to ask what was wrong, but his younger brother hushed him.

"Do you hear that?"

It was soft, somewhere in the far distance, but Zeke couldn't deny it. A low humming, followed by what sounded like a radio transmission. Nodding to his brother, he hurried off in the direction of the sound, Clyde trailing behind him.

They were careful to avoid any cracks and pitfalls, listening intently until the distant sounds became closer. Louder. Echoing off of the debris. And with each *beep* and sputter, a red neon light flashed, atop what appeared to be a tower. A beacon. Drawing Zeke and Clyde closer to what they hoped was life.

When they finally reached the light, beyond the civilization of town, they saw it wasn't attached to a tower. Beneath the blinking red and Zeke's flashlight, titanium reflected.

"It's… a ship," Zeke said quietly, eying the vessel up and down.

It stretched high into the dark skies, faint radio signals echoing from it and filling the silence of the cold morning air. The ship sputtered and hummed again, this time louder than before, causing the ground to tremble and quake beneath it.

"Do you… do you think that…," Clyde began, cut short by the shifting of sand.

Zeke moved the light from the vessel towards the shadows beside him, catching it on an older man – one of the town's advisors. He squinted his eyes at first, allowing them to adjust to the faint light. Once he recognized the brothers, they softened, and a smile spread across his lips.

"Ah! Boys! I was worried you wouldn't have made it."

Zeke slowly lowered his flashlight, still keeping his gaze on the man before him. "We're not too late, are we?"

The man chuckled. "Just in time, actually. You didn't come across any other survivors, did you?"

Zeke shook his head. "None to speak of. Looks like most were lost with the impact…" He paused for a moment. "Did… did anyone else make it out?"

"Plenty," the man said. "They're already on board, all checked in and comfortable. You both should hurry inside and do the same. It's getting so much colder."

Zeke nodded and looked to Clyde, taking hold of his hand and giving it a gentle squeeze. "You're going to be okay…"

The door to the ship opened with a *hiss*, warmth and light escaping from the entrance and flooding the ground around the brothers. They blinked back the brightness, the few hours without sunlight already numbing their eyes and mind. The man motioned them aboard, Zeke making sure that Clyde was careful in his steps. Within the vessel, down the long halls, there was laughter. Life.

Just as quickly as it had opened, the door sealed shut again trapping the cold and darkness outside. With the town that no longer stood. Once again, Zeke ushered his brother forward, this time with a soft smile.

"Come on…"

Clyde glanced over his shoulder for a brief moment, back to the man who radioed in for flight preparation. "Where… where exactly are we going? Will we be safe?"

A grin tugged at the man's lips once again, confidence sweeping across his face. "Of course, little one. There's plenty of abundance for us all there. It's a little planet called Earth, just a few galaxies over. It's a bit of a travel, but once we're there, I assure you that we all will make ourselves right at home."

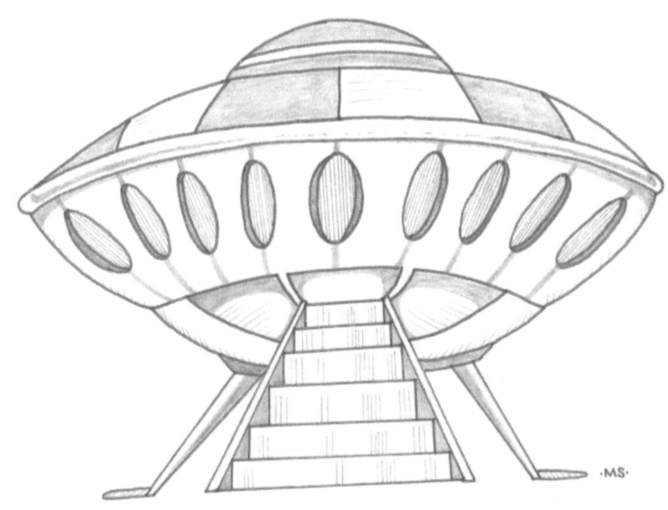

YES
OUI
ABCDEFG
KLM
NOPQRST
XYZ
1234567890
GOOD BYE
BLS

Hello, Brother

Published in 96th October (2020)

You never did like that corner of your room. It was just out of reach from the faint and flickering television—riddled with shadows. I remember your nightly texts, begging me to come over and stay with you until dawn. You said the darkness was too much to bear. That what was waiting within it was watching.

I assured you so many times over the months that you were safe. That the shadows were nothing more than the trick of light. The nights I stayed with you, I would keep a close eye on that corner, on the shadows stirring. And that was all they simply were. Shadows. Yet, no matter how often I tried to comfort you, you told me otherwise.

"Can't you see him?"

You told me in the early hours of morning, you would awake to an added weight on your bed. A man, no, *creature*, smothered in shadow. You'd say he would just sit there and stare through empty voids, examining each one of your movements. Your breaths. But you never saw his face. All you could make out was the heavy stench of decay. Death. Night after night, I would hear the same story. But, yet, each time I stayed with you, the entity never appeared.

"You're tired," I'd say. "Over exhaustion can cause the mind to conjure up shapes in the darkness."

"They're not shapes," you'd interject. "They're real. *He's* real. And he's coming for me."

It wasn't until late November that my suspicion finally grew. You were working the closing shift at your part-time job, bringing you home close to 1am. It certainly wasn't the best paying and the late night hours weren't always reasonable, but you insisted on keeping it. Just until the following spring. You'd chosen to defer your first year of college unlike many of the others who graduated with us just a few months prior to help pay the bills if needed. Your recently separated single father was always working. And any extra help with your younger siblings was enough to ease his mind. So, like you, I deferred, as well; picking up odd jobs during the day until the spring.

I waited in your room, in silence, scrolling through social media on my phone, until you'd come home. When I heard the knock on your bedroom door, just a little past 12, I assumed you'd finished up early. But, it wasn't you. It was your younger brother, Brad—only ten.

"Can I stay in here with you?"

Your brother always looked up to me, so I assumed it was more or less to tell me about his school day or show me videos he was making on his mobile app. But, something about him seemed off. I could sense the fear in his eyes and the quiet way he spoke. He was never one to keep his voice down—not even after family had fallen asleep. It was regular he'd get a scolding: "Dad's in bed, keep it down!" But tonight… He just wasn't himself.

So, of course, I stepped aside and let him in.

When I asked him if everything was okay, he shook his head, gaze to the floor. My initial thought was either a bad dream keeping him awake, bullying in school, or the late night loneliness of a child missing his estranged mother. But, what he uttered was nothing that I was expecting.

"The Woodsman was visiting again…"

At first, I suspected you had been telling these stories to Brad, in hopes to keep him awake at night. You never called it "The Woodsman", but from the description the child provided, I was certain it was the same old story. A dark, shadowed figure that lurked in the corner of the room, getting closer as the night went on. With every blink. Every fading ray of light.

"He comes every night and watches me… And that smell…"

It took me by surprise when you informed me you'd never spoken of the being with your brother. You said, you were too busy with work, or with me, and when you *were* home, he was in school. It was just more evidence, more *proof* that this *thing* was real.

But I'd yet to see it.

I tried thinking back to when you first began mentioning him. When we first started dating, you were so full of happiness and laughter; but now, you were quiet. Solemn. But, when *was* the last time I'd seen you smile? Genuine?

The only night I could think of was in autumn, late October. The night we decided to play that game.

It was the week before Halloween, and I had been spending nearly every day at your house. My schedule was light at work, so I took any earlier shifts that were offered to ensure I would be home with you most of the day. Home just in time to get the kids from school down the street. You came from a decently sized family: your younger brother and twin sisters, Sasha and Sarah, who were just entering their first year of high school. Sasha was much more refined, mature beyond her age. She was quiet, with a borderline Wednesday Addams look to her. Sarah, on the other hand, was far more childish. Bright, loud. Pastel and bubblegum. I often wondered how they could be sisters, let alone twins.

The girls would always be home first, about an hour before the elementary school let out, so most days, they would join us in picking up your little brother.

I remember how crisp the air had been that day. The leaves crunching under our feet as we made our way down the long side streets to the school. We held hands, our body heat keeping each other warm. From behind us, I remember hearing your sisters giggling. Talking in hushed tones. It wasn't until after we picked Brad up that we heard what they were conspiring.

"Dad's working late tonight," Sasha said. "He said he won't be home until at least midnight. We're thinking, why don't we do a little ghost hunting? You know, to kill the time?"

You barked back immediately at your sister. "You know Dad doesn't want any of that in the house. He doesn't even want us *speaking* about—"

"Dude, chill," Sarah chimed in. "Dad's not home until late, can't you hear? He won't even know. Plus, I *know* you've been dying to do it."

She wasn't wrong. You always did have a fascination with the paranormal. Things that couldn't be explained. We'd spent a few times over lunch talking about it: old ghosts in mirrors, cryptids, shadow people. But, I didn't think you would actively *seek* such entities.

"Jade's staying over tonight, too. Come on, it'll be great." Sasha pushed.

You were quiet for a moment longer. I could see it in your eyes that you were leery, but, with a sigh, you agreed.

"Alright, fine. But we cut it at 11, understand? We don't need Dad walking in to any of this."

Sasha and Sarah agreed.

We waited until dark before we began the little game your sisters were so adamant on playing. As soon as the sun sunk behind the hills and the shadows swept across your living room, we gathered.

"The only light we can use is candlelight," Sasha said. "Candles can determine if the spirit is close, and can be used for asking questions."

Your sisters' friend Jade was the one who supplied the candles. Burned down old things that were likely used in games similar to these over the years. She removed her lighter from her back pocket and lit each of the wicks—four candles now flickering in the darkness of the room.

"They represent North, South, East, and West," Jade said. "Or, the elements. Something like that."

"The next thing we need to remember is to watch the time. Both for Dad, and, well, so we don't lose track. Sometimes, when you talk to spirits, you end up trapped in time. They mess with you. Someone has to keep an eye on the clock," Sasha said.

Sarah agreed to be the time keeper.

"We also need to take notes. Anything that the spirits say to us, we need to write down. We can decode it later. They don't always speak in straight sentences… sometimes just broken words. You gotta piece them back together," Sasha continued. "Like a puzzle! Jade will record, as well. We need the audio, just in case there's more than just what's coming through the app…"

"App?" you asked.

Right away, I knew this was nonsense. No one was actually able to speak to the dead through some mobile app. It was most likely something you'd pay $1.99 for and it would generate words when you talked to it—like Siri, only less helpful. But, your sisters claimed otherwise. They were convinced that this app was real. Legit.

"And lastly, no one can speak unless you're the one asking the questions. No whispers, no laughs, nothing. If we're going to pick up what the spirits are trying to say… we have to be silent." Sasha opened her notepad, ready to begin taking notes. "Any questions?"

I, of course, had none. To me, this was silly. The kids were going to scare themselves senseless over random words and phrases their mobile app decided to pull, and actually believe it was true. So, I just sat back, arms folded, and watched as the others took their seats beside me, forming a circle.

"Do… do you really think we're going to talk to a ghost?" Brad asked, huddled up beside me.

"It's just a game," I told him. "You're going to be okay. There's no *real* ghosts."

Once we all were situated, Sasha silenced us, and opened her app.

"Hello?" Sarah wanted to initiate the conversation. "Are there any spirits here that we're connecting with?"

The app was silent for a few moments, but then, the words HELLO, BROTHER appeared across Sasha's screen. From the corner of my eyes, I thought I saw the candles flicker, as if brushed by the wind, but I kept my focus on your sisters.

"Hello brother?" Sasha asked, writing it down. "Whose brother?"

From here, the app began generating random words: ROSE, FALL, SKIN, SNOW.

I sat throughout the game, uninterested, watching as you tried to comfort Brad, who was believing this I think more than your sisters had been. I could tell with each word the phone generated, he was getting more and more anxious. Like everything had been targeted at him personally.

"Hold on, there are some more things coming through…" Sasha held the phone out so we could read it for ourselves.

BEWARE, DEAR.

"Beware… dear?" Sasha repeated. "Dear, who? And… beware *what*?"

JANUARY, 24

Sarah glanced around between us. "Is… that day important to any of you?"

None of us spoke. We just looked amongst ourselves, waiting for an answer. But, of course, none of us could give one. Again, Sasha questioned the app.

"Beware *what*?"

FATHER.

The candles all went out. I'd be lying if I didn't also emit a scream when it happened, but it was lost in that of your sisters, Jade, and Brad. And, of course, you—who turned to laughing as you flicked the light switch on. Of course, at that moment, the front door opened and your father entered, looking exhausted and annoyed after a long day's work.

"What is going on in here?" was all he could ask, eying the candles and the terrified look on Brad's face.

"We were just telling scary stories, Dad, chill," Sasha said.

I could tell he didn't like that answer. And so, he ushered everyone to bed.

Brad turned in for the night immediately, in his room down the hall. The rest of us gathered in Sarah and Sasha's room, reviewing what was written in the notebook and the playback Jade recorded of our session. Sasha laid the notebook out for all of us to see, recounting all the words that the app pulled for her.

HELLO, BROTHER, ROSE, FALL, SKIN, SNOW, BEWARE, DEAR, JANUARY, 24, FATHER…

"Well, when we said hello, the first thing it came back with was 'Hello, Brother'," Jade said. "So, obviously, it *had* to be talking to either you or Brad."

She motioned towards me. I did have a brother—five years younger than me—but he was at home, most likely sound asleep by now. There were no *ghost* siblings that I had. Nor did you or your family. Again, I was convinced, it was just an app pulling words it thought we'd want to hear.

"Beware…," Sasha read quietly. "That whole part just, it's eerie. BEWARE, DEAR. JANUARY 24. But, beware of *what*?"

"Falling? Or snow?" you asked, looking at the words. "Or falling *in* snow?"

"I still think it was creepy how it knew your dad was coming home right before the candles went out," Jade said. "*That*, I'd say, takes the cake tonight."

I did agree that part was a little creepy, but again, it was most likely a coincidence. The kids had left the windows open—so it was likely the late night breeze blew the candles out, and it just happened to be when your dad was pulling into the driveway.

"What about the playback?" you asked. "Is there anything picking up on there?"

Jade hit the replay button, and for a while, we just sat and listened to Sasha and Sarah asking their questions to dead air. None of us spoke, and the app was text only. So, frankly, it was quite boring listening to.

But then, somewhere around the 11 minute mark, there was another sound. Like a low whisper.

"Whoa… what was that?" Sasha asked. "Go back. Was that Brad?"

Jade rewound the recording a few seconds. Brad? No… he had been seated right next to me the whole time. He was silent. Too scared to say a word. The only sound he'd made was a scream when the candles went out—but, we *all* were guilty of that.

Jade replayed the audio, and we all leaned in close and listened. There definitely was a voice in the background static, but what it was saying was indistinguishable. It would fade in and out throughout the rest of the recording, until just before the candles went out. Only then, were the words clear—deep, raspy.

"*I smell the skins…*"

Then, on the audio, we all screamed.

You were the first one to stand up. "Turn it off. Right *now*, Jade."

I glanced over to you, feeling uneasy for what I know we all just heard, but certain that it was something Jade had messed with on her recording app to scare us. I tried to calm you, but that's when I noticed that Sasha was panicking, as well.

"Did it really just say that? 'I smell the *skins*'?"

"What's that supposed to mean?" I asked, immediately thinking of some 80's slasher film cannibal killer, making furniture out of the skin and flesh of his victims.

"Maybe it's a skin walker," you said, looking horrified. "I know you're not supposed to speak of them, but…"

"Shh," Sasha hushed you. "Don't say that! Please!"

The kids didn't sleep that night. To be honest, none of us did. I stayed awake, comforting you, while your siblings huddled together, keeping their eyes on the dark end of the driveway outside their window. When morning came, I assured you all it was just a game on the phone, that we'd all just worked ourselves up into believing we heard what we did, and that there was nothing actually there.

"It's just an app."

"But you heard it," you insisted. "We all did. You can't deny that. You *heard* what it said…"

I was silent for a moment. "What exactly *is* a skin walker?"

You were hesitant, I could clearly see that. But, you trusted me.

"Just… keep quiet about it, okay? We're not supposed to speak of them."

I knew that your family had ties to a reservation out west. You'd mentioned it a couple of times, about how your grandfather left during the war. He met your grandmother overseas, and, well, he gave up most of his tribe's tradition. Passed only a few things down to the later generations: your mother, you, and your siblings. You'd mentioned a few times, on your talks of the unknown and uncanny, that he mainly focused on the stories. The unexplainable parts of the culture. And, now that I thought about it, I vaguely remembered skin walkers being one of those.

"When you talk about them, they become stronger. It's like, your words and thoughts of them attract them. Bring them to you. Something like that," you said. "I don't remember everything. It's kind of like a curse. One that just becomes unbearable. Humans turning into animals, cutting half their lives to be able to become one. And, if they can't become an animal themselves, they take the body of animals nearby. They become monsters. Some of them, even to the point of cannibalism. Always looking for fresh flesh. My grandpa says, he always believed those they loved were the most at risk. The skin walkers would go to them first."

I listened to how sincere your voice was. So quiet… but I could tell you were serious.

"You can tell they're not a normal animal because they walk on two legs—like man. They have no tails. And, often times, you smell rotten flesh when they make themselves known. They're like witches, sort of. Usually, they're a sign of a bad omen… *death*. We don't speak of them."

"Why do you think that's what it is?" I asked. "I mean, I didn't *smell* anything rancid when we were playing the game. I didn't *see* anything like that."

You looked guilty. "I was talking to my grandpa a few weeks ago on the phone. Just… asking questions. About mom. About the stories. Culture. I don't know how it came up, honestly. But we… we talked about them. Maybe he saw something in my future. Or, in a dream… I don't know."

I pulled you close and kissed your forehead. "It's okay. I'm not going to let them hurt you."

You didn't speak of the skin walkers or the game for the next few days. We spent our time picking out Halloween costumes that we would wear when taking Brad around your neighborhood. And loading up on candy and pumpkin spice.

When Halloween night fell, we made our way through your quiet neighborhood, through the shadows and lack of streetlights. Sasha and Sarah used their phones for light, and we trailed behind with flashlights. We'd all agreed on the same theme—forest spirits. You were a stag, with handmade antlers rising from your amber curls, and your sisters were rabbits. I chose a fox, cat ears repainted to fit the design. And Brad—he was a bear. His zip-up onesie was the perfect fit for him—and comfortable, too.

We made our rounds until curfew, gathering up as much candy as we could for your brother. With so many houses on your street, his bucket was overflowing, and he promised each of us a handful when we got back home.

We stayed up for a while and watched scary movies, waiting for midnight. For the end of Halloween and the dawn of what would become Thanksgiving season—or, for others, *Christmas*. Brad turned in to bed before then, and your father fell asleep on the couch. Around 11:30pm, Sasha and Sarah ushered us to their bedroom, figuring it would quieter there—less of a chance to wake their father.

But, when we all sat on their floor, eating away at our piles of candy, I realized it *wasn't* for just sitting around and talking.

Sasha pulled out a spirit board.

"There's no way we're playing that," you insisted. "Sasha… those things are dangerous."

"Look, if you follow the rules, there's nothing to worry about. You played the other game with us last week, didn't you?" she jeered back.

I interrupted. "We played that game and you all freaked yourselves out."

Sasha waved me off. "Pssh. Yeah, and? That's the *point*. Come on. Don't be lame."

Being honest, I'd never played with a spirit board before. Even though I really didn't believe in this stuff, there was something about it that bothered me. Something that kept me away from ever wanting to try. But, when Sasha set it up, hands on the planchette, I felt the need to.

"Shouldn't someone keep notes?" I asked.

"Sarah's got it," Sasha replied. "She's too chicken to play."

"Am *not*," she said. "I'm just way better at taking notes than you."

"Stop arguing," you groaned, placing your hand on the planchette, as well before looking at me. "You… gonna play?"

I sighed and added my hand. "What are the rules?"

"Haven't you seen *any* horror movies?" Sasha sassed. "It's kind of like last time… only the person asking questions can speak. And… no one can play alone. You have to keep your hands on the planchette at all times. And, you have to keep track of the time. You can't let it get away from you. Also… always remember to say 'goodbye'. You have to remember that. And finally, if the board starts counting down to 0, you need to say 'goodbye'. No more questions."

That wasn't so hard, I told myself. Basically, you'd sit there and let your fingertips move the piece on the board to different letters, building an answer that you want to hear. I knew right away that Sasha was going to be spelling things out—trying to make it look like we connected with a spirit.

"First thing's first. We circle the board," she said, moving her hands on the planchette so that we all joined in.

Three times around the board… One, two, three. We stopped in the middle. Sasha looked over at you, nodding.

"Are there any spirits here with us tonight that wish to talk?" you asked.

The planchette remained still. We kept our arms outstretched, watching for any sign of movement. But, there was none. After a few minutes, you repeated your question.

"Are there any spirits here with us tonight that wish to talk?"

Everything was still, but then, slowly, I felt the planchette under my fingertips move. Sasha gasped and looked over at you.

"Are *you* doing that?"

You hushed her. "*No*, of course not. It's probably *you*."

I glanced at them for only a second, before looking back at the board.

H-E-L-LO-B-R-O-T-H-E-R

I felt Sasha pull her hands back for a moment, fingertips still touching the planchette.

"Holy *shit*!" she shrieked.

"Sasha. Language," you said.

"Hello, brother?" Sarah asked, writing it down on her notepad. "Hello… brother… Isn't that the same thing that the app said last time?"

"Sasha, I *know* it was you," you said, glaring across the board at your sister.

"Honest to *God*, it's *not*," she replied.

I hushed everyone and looked back at the board.

"Are you a good spirit?" I asked, my voice low.

At first, I wasn't going to ask any questions. But, for some reason, it kind of just came out of me. The planchette was still again for a moment, but then glided over to the image of the sun on the board.

"Sun?" I asked.

"Yeah, I think that means it's good," Sasha replied.

I looked at the word YES on the board, unsure why that wasn't what was chosen, had that been the case. Perhaps the planchette had overshot, missing the word and landing on the sun. Nevertheless, I shrugged it off and kept playing. You and Sasha asked basic questions back and forth, getting simple YES or NO answers. I had to admit, it was entertaining. Yet, time seemed to tick away, lost to a good hour or so with the board. Around 1am, Sarah spoke up.

"Guys, I think you should ask maybe two or three more questions and call it good. It's getting really late."

I looked down at the letters and at the planchette, and asked, "Is there something that you want to tell us before we go?"

Again, the planchette was still. But then, slowly, once more, it made its way over to begin spelling out words.

B-E-W-A-R-E…

"Beware," I said.

From behind me, I could smell something foul. Almost like old, rotting meat. Or an old dog bone. I tried to ignore it, watching as the rest of the word spelled itself out.

D-E-A-R

"Dear. Beware, Dear," Sarah said as she wrote.

"That's… that's the same thing we heard from the app," you said quietly.

"I think we should say goodbye," I said.

Our hands began to force the planchette down towards the words at the bottom of the board, but with a greater force, we felt it stop at the numbers.

1-2-3…

It was slow at first, and we all watched with intent. Quiet. Until we realized what was happening.

4-5-6…

It was faster now.

7-8…

"Say goodbye!" Sasha yelled.

We used what strength we had to slide the planchette away from the numbers, down to the words "GOOD BYE" at the very bottom of the board.

9- GOOD BYE…

The planchette slid from beneath our fingertips and glided across the wooden floor, under Sarah's bed. We all sat in silence, breathing heavy, before glancing down at the board.

"Sasha…," you said after a few minutes. "Was that you spelling that stuff out? The stuff from the app?"

"No," Sasha said quietly. "Swear on Dad's life it wasn't."

There was a stillness around the house that night, though none of us could sleep. We all remained in your sisters' room, board hidden away in the closet, camping out and watching the shadows on the walls. You had become silent. Staring into the nothingness with empty eyes. Sasha attempted to get your attention once or twice, but to no avail. We assumed it was from shock. From disbelief and fear of what had just happened. And how no one was taking credit for the words that were spelled out on the board.

Only when you rose to your feet and walked out of the room towards the kitchen did we begin to worry.

You stood before the opened fridge, letting the cold light from within flood you. The foul stench from the bedroom—of rotting meat—wafted through the air. Thin at first, but heavy around you.

Cold blood dripped from between your fingers, the sound of raw meat squelching. The thawing steak your father had placed in the fridge overnight was gripped tightly in your hands, torn apart in fatty strings by your teeth. The droplets of red meat blood clung to your lips as your vacant eyes continued to stare into the depths of the fridge. Teeth and nails still tearing away at the hunk of raw meat. Sasha gasped at the sight, yanking you away, and prying the bloodied mass from your fingers.

"What are you doing?" she yelped. "Are you… are you okay?"

You didn't answer her. Your eyes still only remained empty, clouded over, and staring off into the blackness of your bedroom. Sarah watched from afar, cautiously, as Sasha did the only thing she knew.

"Call Paw-Paw."

I stayed in the living room that night, waiting as your sisters shrouded the bedroom in white sage. Your grandfather's voice was muffled on the other end of the phone, but I could sense the fear in his tone. I closed my eyes at some point in the night, praying that whatever it was that befell you would vanish. That, hopefully, you were exhausted from lack of sleep and unaware of what you were doing. This couldn't be a spirit, could it? I kept trying to tell myself that. But with the frantic measures your family was taking, I wasn't so sure anymore.

At around 4am, I glanced back towards your sisters' room, when the voices had finally died down. From the corner of my eye, however, leaning just around the doorframe of your room, I swore that I saw a dark shadow. Standing there. Watching. It was quick, so I was unable to make out any features of a definite shape. But I knew it was there.

I brushed it off as a trick of the mind. After all, I thought, I hadn't slept in almost 24 hours.

It wasn't long after that Sasha and Sarah emerged, heading over to the couch and smiling sadly at me. I hugged them both, reassuring them that everything was okay.

"How is she?" I asked after a moment.

"She's going to be alright," Sasha said. "Paw-Paw knows how to heal things like this."

I looked in at you just to make sure all was well. And, sure enough, your sisters were right. You were wrapped in blankets on their bed, sound asleep. The room was thick in smudge smoke, but to me, it was better than the scent of rotten meat.

I turned to Sasha and motioned towards the closet. "Do you think it was…"

She nodded. "Whatever we connected with… something got through."

Sasha and Sarah agreed that in the afternoon, they'd walk the board to the river and dispose of it.

For a short time, everything seemed to return to normal. You were your bright, bubbly self again. We spent afternoons over coffee and laughed about old memories and stories. I had to hand it to your grandfather… Whatever it was he had told your sisters to do seemed to work wonders. Even if, as I told myself, it was subconscious for you. And it stayed that way, but only for a few weeks.

As autumn faded into the dreary and cold winter, I watched as you became more distant. Silent. You spoke of having nightmares, of seeing that dark figure in your room. How Brad was beginning to see it, too. *The Woodsman…*

You told me the more you looked at it, you could see its basic shape. What looked like long hair covering its face, long and emphasized features. But still all silhouetted in the shadows of your room.

"Sometimes," you'd say, "it almost looks like it has antlers. Kind of like my stag costume on Halloween."

There was a brief amount of time again between the end of December and early January that you didn't speak of the shadows. Of the man in your room. Of the Woodsman. Maybe it was the joy of the holidays—the lights of Christmas and New Year's. Their golden glow illuminated even the darkest corners of the house, and for the first time since mid-November, I saw you smile.

But, it was around the end of January that I began to see your fear again. You weren't eating. You weren't sleeping. The dark circles under your eyes made that clear. And so, I decided to spend a weekend getaway up in the mountains for us at my parents' old cabin. Just enjoying the snow and the peace and the quiet. Getting you away from that house. From your thoughts and your fears.

Your sisters told me that your lack of sleep had been making you distant. All aspects of you fading with the changing of the season. And your hunger—they said if nothing else, you still had an appetite. You'd been eating more than usual, likely to sustain some sort of energy.

I promised them both that the trip away would be good for you. That upon our return, hopefully, you would have gotten enough rest and been able to relax. Far away from the Woodsman and the fear of ghosts. Sasha handed me some dried sage the night before we left.

"Take this," she said. "Just in case…"

The drive was long and the roads more difficult the more we climbed the mountain, but I saw that look in your eyes of content. That maybe you believed everything would be okay. That the nightmares would finally stop.

"How much longer do you think it'll take?" you asked, once we were on the back roads away from towns—surrounded by endless white.

"Oh, probably another hour or so," I replied. "Why?"

"I dunno," you said quietly. "I'm just, starting to get hungry is all."

I reached over and took your hand, giving it a squeeze. You smiled back at me, softly. Had I not looked over and at you, just long enough to see the fading sunset in your eyes, maybe I would have seen it.

From between the trees, out from the mounds of endless snow, a deer emerged—striking the front of my car. You shrieked at the impact, my breaks screeching, car sliding on the powdered snow beneath the tires, driving us down into a ravine of white.

Everything was so blurry. My head spun from shock, and I watched as you began to breathe heavily. Likely a panic attack coming on. I reached my trembling hand out to you again, resting it against your knee. But you pushed me away.

"I-I need fresh air…," you stammered. "Everything's just so… so dark. I just need air…"

You undid your seat belt and opened the door, squeezing out and heading towards the road. To where I knew the carcass of the deer lay. My breath was still shaky, as well, and I scrambled for my phone to call for help. I knew service would be blotchy up there, but if I managed to get ahold of someone for help, even if it took a while, it was better than nothing. After all, the sun was almost down over the ridges now—and soon, the shadows would start to cover the land.

I was able to connect with the police, reporting the accident and informing them that we were both okay, just shaken up, but that we were remaining with the car. They estimated about a half hour or so, depending on how heavy the snowfall became. The flurries now were enough to make the roads slick, but thankfully not enough to hinder sight. At least, not yet.

Once I disconnected from the call, I glanced down at the screen of my phone, and the date and time that displayed.

January 24th, 4:38pm.

January 24th. That date stuck out in my head for some reason. More-so than just our trip. But why, I just couldn't pinpoint. I just looked out ahead of me, out at the steadily falling snow.

Fall. Snow.

That old, rancid smell of rotten meat—of *death*—began to creep back into my nostrils. And my blood began to run cold.

January 24.

Beware, dear.

Deer.

My heart raced against my chest as I glanced in the rear view mirror, looking out over the ditch and into the road. I unbuckled my seatbelt and hurried outside, looking for you. To tell you that maybe, just maybe, those little games were more than coincidence. But, when I got to the roadway, there was nothing there. No you, no deer. A faint pool of blood where the animal had bled out was all that was left. And next to it… a pile of your clothes.

I stepped closer, inspecting it, before I heard your heavy, panicky breaths behind me. On my neck. Hot. Wet. With each breath you emitted, I smelled that rotten stench again. The foul, lingering scent of flesh. And in the setting sun, I watched as your shadow stretched out above mine. Long, dark, emphasized. With antlers—those stag antlers from Halloween.

There was a low, guttural groan as you opened your jaw, before whispering to me in your honeyed voice. Sad, but yet, confident. Breathy. Sinister. As I turned to face you, your words echoed through the winter wind on the mountain, caught in the flurry of snow.

"Hello, brother…"

MARK
SINNOTT

·MS·

Shadows and Sparks

Published in Dreich Magazine (2021)

You visit me in candle flame,
flickering bodies dancing so bright;
bewitched against the canvas of shadow—
in golden and amber light.

Do you remember me,
the breath of air that birthed your spark;
the one who fed the embers—
and silenced the ever-deep dark?

And do you search for me,
in ghosts that haunt the walls;
in melancholy mementos—
asking, would you change it all?

I've watched the wax drip softly,
and the wick burn down in time;
convinced that even when snuffed out—
the fire is still mine.

And as the smoke rises slowly,
and the darkness bleeds anew;
do you sit in the silence and wonder—
if those shadows belong to you?

BLS

The Beast of Cupola Pond

Read on Believing the Bizarre (2021)

Growing up in Ripley County, I was familiar with the tales. The warnings whispered through our small town – on playgrounds, in hardware stores, and on the local evening news. How many townsfolk had gone missing over the years. Lost late in the night. Disappearing in thin air. That is, however, until their mangled bodies were found. Gnawed down to the bone. Left to boil under the hot summer sun in Cupola Pond.

Some said it was a deranged killer hiding out in the Ozarks – picking off residents one by one. But there was no string of evidence. No traits that linked each victim to one another. The deaths were random. Gruesome. And they always seemed to happen monthly. Around the rise of the full moon.

"It's a werewolf for sure," my friends would say. "Just like in the movies."

But I didn't believe it. The "Full Moon Murderer" – as our town had dubbed them – was no more than a mere man. Out for blood. Fueled by the adrenaline of the kill. Still though, they swore up and down it was a monster. A werewolf hiding out in the thick marsh groves. How infantile they were. Caught up in their fantasies.

Back and forth we bickered that summer. Of fictitious monsters in comic books and magazines. On the big screen. Davey, Ben, and Sam stood firm with their belief. As I did mine. I assured them their imaginations were merely running rampant. That they were too caught up in their late night monster flicks. That there were no wolves in our town. Or the swamp. And I was so certain of it, that I made the suggestion to head into the swamp late that Friday evening. On the last night of the full moon.

During the summer, Cupola was a breeding ground for blackflies. The air was hot and sticky, and insects buzzed through the dark murk of the trees and water. When the rainy season had passed, most of the earth was dry – save for mounds of mud far out beneath the river birches. But after a good summer storm, the bog waters were high. Covering much of the low vegetation and mossy twigs and stones. And how convenient those rains always seemed to be. Heaviest just days before the peak of the full moon. Making it easy to hide bodies beneath the dark water to decompose.

"Are you sure this is a good idea?" Davey asked, stepping over a fallen log. "My dad's gonna be pissed if—"

"I just want to prove to you there's no werewolf," I replied. "That way, you guys can stop carrying on about it. I'm tired of this nonsense."

"And what if we *do* see one?" Ben piped up. "And we prove *you* wrong?"

I paused and then sighed. "Then I give you permission to rag on me for the rest of the summer, okay?"

"Pssh." Ben scoffed with a smirk. "Deal."

Aside from the sounds of insects and frogs playing their nightly chorus beneath the trees, the swamp was still. The mud squelched under our feet as we headed deeper through the groves, waving away the late night gnats. They were always the worst after the rains came. Flocking to the swamp water for hydration – festering in the heat. I shone my flashlight across the algae covered waters, watching as waves of steam billowed from the surface. Remnants of the sweltering summer sun. And with it, the lingering stench of mud and decay swept across the land. Snaking through the trees and catching our nostrils. The further we went, too, the heavier it became.

"So," Davey said after a while, "I know we're out here and all to… see if this werewolf is real or… just a story, but… Do you guys really think the stories are true? I mean, about the people going missing? Bodies being found out here?"

"Of course they're true," Sam said, shining her flashlight off between the moss covered trunks of old bald cypresses. "The news covers these stories practically monthly. Remember Mr. Doyle?"

"The bus driver?"

"Yeah, him. Remember they had to have someone else cover his route for weeks last year? No one knew where he was. He never called in to work. Never told family anything… Police searched for a while. Few weeks later, they found him out here. Limbs chewed off. Throat torn open… I mean, that was what they were able to make of what the swamp hadn't done to him, anyway. But yeah. He was out here under the water. Just waiting for the dry spell to expose him. Uncover what was left of him."

"That's why I'm saying it's a werewolf, man," Ben said. "It's always around the full moon. And the bugs aren't out there eating away at him. At least, not eating through *bone*."

"Maybe there's alligators," Davey replied. "You never know."

"We're too far north," I said. "Though, that's more believable than your werewolf theory."

"I'm still holding on to that one 'til the day I die," Ben said. "Cross my heart. I know it's a werewolf."

The light of the moon barely graced the branches of the trees as we trudged along – deeper into the groves and mudflats of Cupola Pond. As the night went on, shadows growing heavy as they approached the midnight hour, the sounds of life began to drain from the bog. Out here, the frogs had silenced themselves – water likely too deep. And even the insects had quieted. The sudden onset of peace was almost unnerving – especially as we approached the old cabin set off just out of reach from the swamp water. Nestled between the bald cypress.

"Oh shit," Sam whispered, "isn't that Old Man Grady's place?"

I shone the flashlight in the direction of the cabin – its windows dark save for the light reflecting off the glass from the full moon. I'd forgotten that Old Man Grady lived out on the swamp. Alone. Far away from all of us in the surrounding towns.

My father always said he was a loner – for as long as anyone had known him. A loner, and an odd man at that. Every so often, he'd come into town in his beat up old rusted Ford truck, yammering about the catfish out by his place. How they'd made good meals and were far cheaper than that "overpriced restaurant plate" price local scratch kitchens would charge. He'd only show himself for the essentials. Oil for his truck, bullets for his hunting rifle, and a pack of cigarettes. Milk, bread, and a bag of potatoes. And dog food, of course. For his old short haired pointer. He'd light his cigarette, take a long drag, fill up his can of oil, and be on his way. Back out to the swamp he isolated himself within. Emerging from only once a month.

Once a month...

"Old Man Grady's a weird one," Ben said. "You know, I wouldn't be surprised if he were our werewolf."

"Heck," Sam said, "I'd peg him as the Full Moon Murderer whether or *not* he's a werewolf."

"You think he's in there?" Davey asked, motioning towards the cabin.

I shone my light back in its direction, focused heavily on the black windows. From just beyond the reach of my flashlight's ray, I could see his rusted truck parked alongside the cabin. So, unless he had been out late night fishing or hunting, I was certain he was there. Likely sound asleep.

"We should get going," I said softly.

"Get going?" Ben raised an eyebrow. "What do *mean* get going? This was *your* idea, Lee. Since you're so adamant to prove there isn't a werewolf."

"Look," I said, "it's getting late. It's wet out here. The bugs are atrocious. And we're on Old Man Grady's property. We don't need to wake him up."

"Who says we're waking him up? We'll be quiet," Ben replied.

"What if we wake his dog up?" I responded. "Then *he's* going to wake up."

"He's right, Ben," Sam said. "And Old Man Grady's crazy. With our luck, he'd end up shooting us or sending his dog to track us down – thinking we're some wild animal."

"Maybe that's what he does...," Davey said quietly.

We glanced over to him. His gaze was focused out in the swamp – in the deep darkness of the low hanging trees and moss. In the faint reflections of white moonlight on the murky water.

"Maybe people come out here looking to see if there's a werewolf. Or, to see if they catch the killer. Maybe he waits out here and hunts them down. Shoots them when they get too close. Cuts them up and turns them into stew and feeds the bones to his dog. Then, whatever's left, he tosses out there in the swamp. For nature to take."

I felt a chill run down my back at Davey's words, but I told myself they weren't true. They couldn't be. Old Man Grady was weird – everyone in Ripley County knew that – but he wasn't a murderer.

"That's probably why he only needs to come to town once a month. He stocks up on a good portion of meat. Catches his catfish. Makes his potatoes. It's Old Man Grady. I know it is."

"Either way," Sam said, "werewolf or Old Man Grady or the county just making this stuff up… I'm out. It's wet. It stinks. And it's almost midnight. Our parents are going to lose their shit if they catch us not in bed."

She pushed ahead of us, shining her flashlight down the poorly marked trail we had come from. I looked back at Ben and Davey and sighed. With a nod, I turned to join her.

"We'll try again another night."

"But it has to be the full moon," Ben snapped. "You just don't want to be caught being wrong."

"I said we'll try again *another* night, Ben," I replied. "If you want to stay out here and wait for Old Man Grady to chew you out… be my guest. But I'm going home."

I started back after Sam, feet sliding on the mud. The sounds of buzzing insects began to rise again in the sticky heat of the night, and I could barely make out Davey's pleads with Ben to go home. I waved away a swarm of gnats, blinking hard to keep them from landing on my eyelashes. They were everywhere. Out there in the hot swamp water. Laying eggs. Preparing for the next generation to infest Cupola.

With another step, I felt cool water seep into the soles of my shoes. Bubbling up from the mud. I groaned at the feeling, my feet sloshing around inside my now drenched shoe as I followed behind Sam. All I could make out of her was her flashlight – farther ahead through the groves of trees. And still, I didn't bother looking back for Davey or Ben. If they chose to stay out there all night and look for that "werewolf" of theirs, then so be it. But I wanted no part. Especially if it meant trespassing on Old Man Grady's property.

I continued forward along the path for a little longer until I heard the heavy stamping of footsteps behind me. I shone my light back down the path, catching sight of Davey and Ben hurrying after me. Mud flew up from beneath their shoes as they scrambled, eyes wide and breathing labored. I raised an eyebrow as they approached.

"What's going on?" I asked.

Ben struggled to catch his breath as he pointed a shaky finger out towards the waters of the swamp. "The werewolf… he's out there… We saw him…"

I blinked in disbelief, turning my attention to Davey who merely nodded in agreement. "Swear to God."

"You can't be serious," I said. "You guys must have seen something else. A tree or a deer or something."

"I think we know what a *tree* and a *deer* look like, Lee," Ben snapped. "It was a werewolf. Big. Hairy. On two legs. Standing out there across the swamp. Come look for yourself."

"What about Sam?" I asked.

"Davey will go get her. Just come with me," Ben urged. "Before it's gone."

I took a deep breath, but followed him. My suspicions were still high, convinced there was no way there was a werewolf living out here. Not in Ripley County. Not in the swamp. Not at all. But the fear that had overtaken my friends worried me. Deep down in my gut. I knew they'd seen something. And whether that had been their "werewolf" or not, it was enough to send them running down the trail after us. Through the mud and the dark.

When Ben and I got back to where he claimed the werewolf was, I saw nothing. The night air was still aside from the humming insects and distant chatter of frogs. There was no movement in the water, nor in the trees and surrounding vegetation. I shone my flashlight out across the dark water – eying the algae and murk. But there was nothing.

“There’s nothing out here, Ben,” I started, “where did you say you saw—”

I felt Ben’s hands roughly shove my shoulders, causing my feet to give way in the slippery mud. Before I had a moment to think, I was down. Face first in the shallow swamp water that had pooled beside the trail. The stale taste of musk overtook my tongue as I spat the water and mud from my mouth, wiping away any remnants of algae from my face. Ben cackled from the path as he shook his head, watching as I emerged from the bog – now soaking wet.

“What the hell, Ben?”

Sam’s voice carried from the trail, her flashlight catching on me. I squinted as the beam of light hit my eyes and I dabbed away at them again with the feeling of the swamp water blinding them.

“Oh come on, Sam,” Ben chucked. “Everyone’s been so damn serious out here tonight. We needed a good laugh.”

“I’m done,” I muttered, droplets of water flicking from my lips. “I’m going home and I’m *not* coming back out here.”

“Oh stop, Lee,” Ben groaned.

“No. This is *stupid*,” I shot back. “We shouldn’t have even been out here anyway. And for what reason were we even? Because we were looking for a *werewolf*? Give me a *break*!”

I shrugged my shoulders hard, letting more droplets of water fall from them as I gave my arms a shake. Though the water in the swamp had been warm, it was becoming cold in the night air. Clinging to my skin and sending chills deep into my bones.

“Werewolves aren’t real. They’re just myths. Folklore. Things in comic books and horror movies,” I said. “There’s no werewolf killing people in Ripley County. So if you’ll excuse me, I’d like to go home and get warm and dry and go to bed.”

Ben didn’t have anything to say to that. I pushed passed him, hearing my shoes squelch as water shot out from the tiny air holes on the top and in my soles. I kept my flashlight steady on the path before me with one hand, tucking my other beneath my elbow to try and keep warm. The gnats and blackflies swarmed even more to me now that I stunk like the muddy swamp. But I ignored them as best I could. I just wanted to be home. Back in bed. Warm. Away from Cupola Pond and away from Ben.

It wasn't long down the path, however, that the beam of my flashlight picked up on something. There was movement through the vegetation ahead – just out of reach from the light. Still, I shone it in the direction, expecting to find a possum or raccoon who had come down from the trees for a midnight stroll. But there was nothing. Nothing except the dark silhouette that I could just barely make out – standing directly in the path.

At first, I thought it was Old Man Grady. Awoken by our shouts and childish behavior. But the more I squinted and tried to make out features in the shadows, the more I realized it couldn't have been him. At least, not *human* Old Man Grady.

The body was too large – muscular. And it appeared to be hunched over, as if walking on knuckles. Or, all fours. Then, I thought of Old Man Grady's dog. But, this was far too big to be a hunting dog.

I heard the squishing of mud behind me as my friends approached. Diverting the ray of my flashlight, I hushed them, motioning towards where the silhouette stood.

"Look," I whispered. "Do you see that?"

And sure enough they did. I felt Sam's fingers dig into my arm as she stared out at that big, black shadow. And Davey's rapid breaths were certainly out of fear.

"What is it?" Sam asked quietly.

I shook my head. "I-I don't know…"

Through the shadows and low lying fog that began to drift out from across the swamp water, we could see a pair of red eyes glow. Like headlights. Coming from the bulky body of the beast. And then, that sound. A sound I'll never forget… From its throat emerged a deep, bellowing howl. Like nothing we had ever heard. It was low – yet high – and it rattled our bones as it drifted through the trees. Riding on the fog. But before we could react, it took off running. Out into the deep groves of bald cypresses and vegetation. Deeper into the bog.

Gripping our flashlights tight, we bolted down the path. Sloshing through the mud and rising swamp water. Not once looking back, even when the howls echoed from the deep distance.

"I told you," Ben said the next morning. "I told you it was a werewolf."

"We don't know that for sure," I replied. "It could have been a bear or something."

"Bears don't live out here," Sam said. "It's just as believable as Davey's alligator theory."

"But we still don't know it was a *werewolf*. Come on. It just doesn't seem plausible."

"You saw and heard the same thing we did, Lee," Ben said. "No animal I've ever seen had glowing red eyes. Hell. It even *howled*! What more proof do you need?"

I paused in thought. As much as I hated to admit it – Ben was right. There was no other way we could have described what we saw. Even if only through shadow. The body was far too big to be a dog. And those eyes. No animal had eyes like that. I then remembered the sound it made. That deep howl. Like a wolf and an elk combined. Rattling the trees and the swamp water.

"Who do you think it is?" I asked softly.

"Old Man Grady. No doubt," Ben said. "He's weird enough as it is. Hiding away out there in the swamp all by himself with his dog. Only leaving to come back here once a month for supplies. It's probably when he hunts. Picks off his victims. Lures them out there and takes care of them under the moonlight."

"So what are we going to do about it?" I asked. "Our parents will never believe us."

"Maybe the police," Davey suggested. "They did say if anyone had any leads on the murders to let them know."

"But will they really think it's a werewolf?" I inquired. "I just… I feel like they're going to tell us we're just kids. Watching scary movies or reading too many comics. They won't believe it."

"You didn't believe it either, did you?" Sam asked.

I was silent. Part of me still didn't want to believe. But I couldn't deny what I had seen. There was no other explanation.

"We'll just have to show them, then," Sam said.

"But how?" I asked. "If we go in there telling them it's a werewolf and to follow us out to the swamp… they'll never do it."

"What if we get a picture?" Sam suggested. "If we can get proof of what we saw and bring it to them… they'll *have* to believe us."

"But that means we have to go back out there," Davey said. "And if it's still lurking around…"

"What if we get photos of the footprints?" Ben piped up. "If we go back during the day, we won't run into it, right? They only come out – erm, *change* – under the light of the full moon. If the sun's up, there won't be a werewolf."

"But there'll be Old Man Grady," Davey said. "And if he's really the werewolf… I know he saw us last night."

"He's too much of a hermit to probably leave his cabin." Ben waved him off. "Besides, what's the worst he'd do?"

I hesitated, but then spoke up. "I can get my camera and we head down there this afternoon. Just before evening. The mud was thick enough that any footprints left behind should still be there. Unless, the swamp water rose and covered them."

"There wasn't any rain, though," Sam said. "We should be able to still see them."

"And, if Old Man Grady comes out and sees us and wants to know what we're doing… just say it's for a project for summer school. He doesn't have to know. Just… taking photos of local vegetation and trees. The ecosystem of the Ozarks."

"You think he'll buy it?" Davey asked.

"If he doesn't, it doesn't matter," Ben said. "By then, we'll have whatever evidence we need to bring back to the police and prove to them that we have a werewolf out in Cupola Pond."

The flies were far worse during the day than at night. They buzzed relentlessly against our ears, humming out across the hot and steamy waters of the swamp. The frogs croaked far out in the middle from fallen, moss covered logs. And birds chattered from treetops – their wings beating against the sticky air. The earth was alive. Not as still and desolate as the night before.

I kept my camera close to my chest as I led my friends through the muddy paths. The mounds of slippery sod squelched beneath our feet as we searched for tracks left behind by the beast – and any sign of movement through the trees. Though everything was brighter and livelier, there was still a heavy feeling of darkness hiding deep in the groves. The feeling that something was watching us from far out in the bald cypresses. Deep in the bog.

As we rounded the corner, we found the area on the path where we had spotted the creature the night before. Just on the bend. At the edge of the fallen and dipping trunks of river trees. I motioned towards the area.

"There," I said. "That's where we saw it."

Approaching, I was careful to avoid the muddy areas in case of contaminating any evidence we may have found. And sure enough, we found plenty. There, preserved in the Cupola mud were deep pairs of footprints. *Paw prints*. Large. Clawed. Inhuman.

"Right there." I pointed to the tracks as Davey, Sam, and Ben surrounded me. "That's gotta be them, right?"

Ben nodded. "Absolutely."

"*Look* at those!" Davey exclaimed. "They're *huge*."

"That thing must have been way bigger than we thought," Sam said. "They look almost like bear prints."

"But there are no bears here," Ben added. "We went over this earlier, remember?"

"Maybe one migrated," I said. "My dad's said he's seen them in the Ozarks before. They could have come down from the more forested areas. It's not impossible."

"But out here in the swamp?" Ben shook his head. "And bears' eyes don't glow."

"I'm just trying to be logical," I said, pointing my camera at the paw prints in the mud and taking a photo. "And, I'm thinking of what the police are likely going to say. Because you and I *both* know that they're not going to believe our story about a werewolf. Regardless of what we saw."

"*Werewolf*?"

I froze at the scratchy, twangy voice behind us. Turning around, my heart pounded heavy against my chest when my eyes met the sunken grey pair of Old Man Grady. His rifle was slung over his shoulder, hunting cap pulled down to prevent the flies from clinging to his salty sweat. At his side was his short haired pointer dog. Sniffing the air – fur on his back raised.

We didn't know what to say. I stammered a few times, gripping my camera tight as I watched him approach. He nudged us aside, glancing down at the prints left in the mud. Rubbing his grey stubbly chin, he thought audibly.

"Hmm…" Old Man Grady turned to face us once again. "You kids say you seen a werewolf?"

Davey meekly nodded. "Y-yes sir. Out here last night…"

"And you be thinkin' those are its tracks?"

"Y-yes sir…"

There was a harsh chuckle from Old Man Grady's throat. And then a hacking wheeze. He waved us off and shook his head.

"There ain't no werewolf out here," he said. "But what you reckon you seen… that wasn't just the shadows either."

"What do you mean?" I asked.

"Is it a bear?" Sam inquired.

"No bear," Old Man Grady said. "No bear indeed. Why, I don't think a bear could outfight that ol' beast."

"Beast?" Ben asked.

Old Man Grady's eyes went cold. "The Howler."

I heard the sound from the night before circling my head. Pricking at my ears. That deep, bellowing howl. The sound the creature made just before darting off into the groves. Out further into the swamp.

"Ya'll heard its call, didn't you?"

I nodded slowly. "Y-yes."

"What… exactly is the *Howler*?" Sam asked.

"No one really knows. Some say it's just a legend. Old myth thought up by the hermits out here to keep away trespassers." Old Man Grady shot us a stern look. "Nosey kids sneakin' out at night where they shouldn't be."

We winced at that. But Old Man Grady shook his head, continuing on.

"But others know the truth. They seen its shadow in the swamp waters. Heard its call echo from beyond the trees. Down from the hills. Out on the lake. They seen its red eyes burn through the night. Felt the hot breath and stench 'a decay. Seen those horns that rise from its skull."

He looked back at the tracks in the mud. After a moment of thought, he whistled, calling his dog to his side. The pointer sniffed the paw prints deeply before emitting a growl in his throat. Old Man Grady nodded.

"Those who seen it say it looks like a mixture 'a boar, bear, wolf, and cat. But with curled horns on its head. A sign it rose up from Hell itself. Here to hunt down wanderin' souls and claim 'em for the Devil."

"Have you ever seen it?" Davey asked.

Old Man Grady was quiet for a moment. "Once. Many years ago. When I was out huntin'. Been spendin' my time out here tryin' to track it down."

"Is that… what's been killing off the people in town?" I asked.

"I reckon it is. That beast shows no remorse. Wanders the Ozarks in the dead 'a night. Pickin' off poor bastards."

"Do the police know?" I held my camera tight to my chest.

Old Man Grady waved me off. "Them police got so much to worry 'bout… they don't got time for ol' myths. And if they ain't never seen it… they ain't gonna believe it."

"We got some pictures of the tracks," I said. "What if we show those to them?"

"They'll need more proof than that," Old Man Grady said. "I tried tellin' 'em years ago, but they never listed. Called me crazy. You best just mind yer business and go on home."

"But—"

"Ya'll heard me," Old Man Grady barked. "There ain't nothin' out here that could convince 'em there's a beast. Now get on goin' back home and don't let me find ya'll out here again on my property."

We remained still for a moment, wanting to inquire further. But Old Man Grady's expression was stern. I gripped the sides of my camera tightly before sighing, motioning my friends to follow. And so, hesitantly, we thanked Old Man Grady and began back down the path we had come from. Back towards the entrance to Cupola Pond. From over my shoulder, I could still feel Old Man Grady's eyes watching us, though. Seeing us off. Ensuring that we wouldn't come back.

"Do you believe that story?" Sam asked as she stepped over an upturned and exposed root. "About the Howler?"

"We saw *something* out here last night," Davey replied. "Why shouldn't we believe him?"

"What if it's a cover up?" Ben asked. "You know… him saying it's this beast roaming out here but really it's him. Changed under the light of the moon."

"Don't tell me you're still on that werewolf kick," I groaned.

"I'm not taking the possibility off the table just yet," Ben said. "Besides. Why else do you think he'd want us out of here so soon? The sun's setting in a few hours. Kind of suspicious, no?"

"He's an old crabby hermit," I said. "He doesn't want people traipsing around his swamp. Especially kids. And if we end up telling the police and they send more search parties out here?"

Sam nodded in agreement. "I mean, yeah… I can't blame him."

"I still say he's hiding something," Ben said. "Or he's just making up the beast thing to cover for himself."

"For the last time, Ben..." I rubbed my temples irritably. "There are no such things as werewolves."

A long, bellowing howl broke through the trees. All at once, silence overtook the swamp. The chatter of frogs and insects died down to a low drone. Barely audible. My breath caught in my throat as I froze in fear – the chill of the sound grating down my back. Deep in my bones. And I could see the others had tensed up, as well.

"D-did you hear that?" Davey asked.

I hushed him. The silence clung for another moment or so before a second howl picked up on the hot summer air. Closer than before. Only this time, it was followed by vicious barking. Growls. Old Man Grady's short haired pointer.

"What should we do?" Sam whispered.

As much as my heart wanted to run, my legs wouldn't budge. It was as though they were sinking into the thick mud. Immobile. Stuck. But I knew it was the fear. It was numbing. And with each sound that rose up from down the path, the more paralyzed I became.

The growls and barks of Old Man Grady's dog were growing louder. Closer together. Frantic. And then, there was gunfire. One loud echo of a rifle. Only then did I jump. Blinking back the blinding fear that had overtaken my vision. Again, the barks trailed down the path. Angry and aggressive. Stopped only when an ear piercing roar shook the trees and made the swamp water bubble. And then, between another shot, the pained yelps of the short haired pointer. But they were only momentary. Once they ceased, silence overtook the swamp again. That was, until we heard heavy footsteps heading our way.

Old Man Grady appeared down the path, rifle gripped tightly as he staggered through the mud. His hunting cap was no longer on his head – thinning grey hair now exposed. A thick line of blood ran from his temple down his cheek as he panted.

"Get on outta here!" he hollered.

But our feet were planted deep in the sod. Our legs trembled, but wouldn't move. We were too in shock. In disbelief. Another roar rattled the cypresses as Old Man Grady looked back over his shoulder. With a wheeze, he aimed his rifle down the dim lit path he had come from.

"You kids go home!" he called out to us again. "By the love 'a God… go home…"

From within the shadows, a pair of red eyes shone. Beady but bright. A low growl rumbled from out of the darkness, and then, we saw it. That bulky, beastly figure from the night before. Emerging into the faint sunlight.

The creature was just as Old Man Grady had described. A large, hulking bear-like body with a wolf-like face. Only its snout was much wider – eyes cat-like and reflective in the light. Their red tint stood out against the beast's thick black fur. Its bottom fangs protruded from saliva dripping gums, exposed over its bottom lip like boar tusks. And from its head, those curled horns rose. Catching the rays of the sun. It took a heavy breath, hot steam blowing from its nostrils as it eyed Old Man Grady, bearing its large, bloodied fangs as it slunk closer. Hunching itself down. Stalking its prey.

Old Man Grady took aim with his rifle and then fired. The beast emitted a shriek as the bullet tore through the flesh of its shoulder – but it continued forward. Though blood began to rise to the surface of the wound, it was hardly an injury to the creature.

Though still stunned, my mind raced. Taking in all that I could see. There it was. The Howler. Standing on the path before us in plain sight. Exposed. The proof we needed… I managed to raise my camera with trembling hands, snapping a photo as the flash lit up the path. The beast blinked back the bright light, before emitting another monstrous roar. And then, in rage, it lunged. Right towards Old Man Grady.

"Run!"

His voice hit our ears as the rifle unloaded the last of its shots. I shut my eyes – afraid to watch the scene unfolding around me. And then, I felt the courage to do what Old Man Grady had commanded. To run.

I pulled my feet from the gripping mud, hurrying down the path and back towards the entrance of the swamp. Davey, Sam, and Ben weren't far behind me. Their shoes squelched in the mud as mind did – slipping and sliding through the bog as our hearts pounded against our chests. I could feel it beating in my ears as I pushed forward – adrenaline pumping through my veins. I gasped for breath with each footfall, but I didn't dare stop. None of us did.

From behind us, the roars of the Howler filled the evening air. And then, Old Man Grady's screams. But still, we didn't stop. We didn't look back. Not even when the silence fell hard again, leaving only the sounds of our distress.

It took a few weeks for the swamp water to drain after the heavy rains that month, but the police eventually found Old Man Grady's body. It was buried out in the mudflats, caked in rotten blood and algae. His torso had been ripped open, legs chewed off, and face torn. Another victim for the "Full Moon Murderer" – at least, according to the police.

"It's such a shame," my father said. "That poor old man was just out there minding his own business. Never harmed anyone. Who would do such a thing?"

I wanted so badly to tell my parents of what we saw. Show them the photos of the footprints on my camera. Of the Howler. But I knew they would be skeptical. Just as I had been.

"Those are bear footprints, honey."

"And that photo? It's blurry as anything. But likely just a bear."

And then I'd be lectured how a bear couldn't do what had been done. That it wouldn't target people in the county. Drag them out to the swamp waters. I knew what I saw. We all did. But even Old Man Grady had tried convincing the town of the Howler once. And it's what drove him away. Drove him out to the swamp to find the creature himself. To hunt it. Prove he wasn't crazy.

I never deleted those photos of what we saw.

It was a long while before any other people went missing in our county after Old Man Grady. Some believed the killer had grown tired of his monthly duties. Others said he had moved on out of the Ozarks and settled north somewhere out on the farmlands. And then there were those who believed it had been Grady himself who was the true Full Moon Murderer. Hiding out in Cupola Pond and luring his victims in after his monthly visits to town. Finally getting picked off by someone who had caught on to him. Delivering him his own fate. A taste of his own medicine.

But I knew better. I had seen it with my own eyes. Heard its cries with my own ears. We all had. And it was injured – Old Man Grady had gotten it good. I was certain it had slunk off into the hills. Back to its den in the caves. A place to hide and rest and recover. And so, I did my best to forget about the Howler. Forget about those who had disappeared in the swamp. Forget about the stories. Life simply returned back to the way things had been.

Yet, late in the night that following spring, I swore I heard it again. Calling from out in the dark swamp waters. That bellowing howl from the summer. That sound I could never forget.

I rose to my feet and walked over to my window, pulling back the curtains and gazing out into the endless darkness of night. Out across my front lawn. Towards the line of trees just beyond our property. And at first, I thought I was just seeing things. But the longer I stared, the more I knew I wasn't. They were there. I was sure of it. Those two red eyes glowing through the trees. Burning. Deep and bright like the fires of Hell.

It had been months, I thought, since anyone had gone missing. Months since the last body had been found beneath the waters and mud of Cupola Pond. But now, I knew that time was up. The Howler had returned. And it had found its prey.

Down to the Filter

All he asked for was a pack of cigarettes. The cheapest I could find. He was easy to please. And so, I laid them on the nightstand, accompanied by a gin and tonic – something extra for his hard work – and waited for the shadows. The darkest part of night. The very essence I had come to embrace.

But, the shadows weren't always my friend…

I'd often swore it was the bottle my husband was wed to. Countless nights he'd nurse at the neck, shouting sour words off his serpentine tongue. Coated in that thick liquid. Bitter. Cruel. It had been years since I'd heard a kind word. Any sense of endearment or love. All of our misfortunes, all of our shortcomings… *I* was to blame. The lost money. The late bills. The missing mortgage. The further into debt we fell, the bigger the bottle became. And the harsher the words. I was at the end of my rope…

Until I met *him*.

It was late in the night at Cici's Diner – the only escape. He sat in the shadows at the end of the bar, cigarette tip glowing as he puffed thick rings. At first, I paid him no mind. But the feeling of being watched burned through my back and I couldn't help but look towards him. Look into those fiery eyes fixated on me so well. Interlocking deep within my soul. Unwavering.

He uttered not a word. Yet, still he stared. And his smile grew ever wider. Droll lips drawn up to reveal straight, white teeth. I tried my best to ignore him. To keep his grinning image out of my mind. I sipped my coffee and looked vacantly into the empty seat across from me. But still I could feel them. Those burning eyes. Searing away at me.

A little before dawn, he rose from his barstool. His shiny black shoes clapped against the floor as he made his way to the door. But, of course, not before stopping beside my booth. The heavy scent of smoke stung my nostrils as he stood over me, holding out his card.

“Should you ever need assistance…”

I took it hesitantly, keeping my vision on my mug. Not daring to look up and face him. He took a long, final drag on his cigarette before mashing it out in the ash tray at my table. And then, he was gone. Lost to the rising sun.

I awoke to the sound of sirens echoing through the early morning. The wavering flashes of red and blue. Up I sat, eyes wide in the dim light, struggling to adjust to the shadows. All around me, I could smell that smoke. Taste the salt thick in the air. Downstairs, the paramedics radioed in for backup. Their patient *Dead on Arrival*.

I glanced over to my nightstand, noticing the pack of cigarettes was gone. The gin and tonic drank dry. In their place was only his card, name vivid in the faint morning sun. LUCIFER.

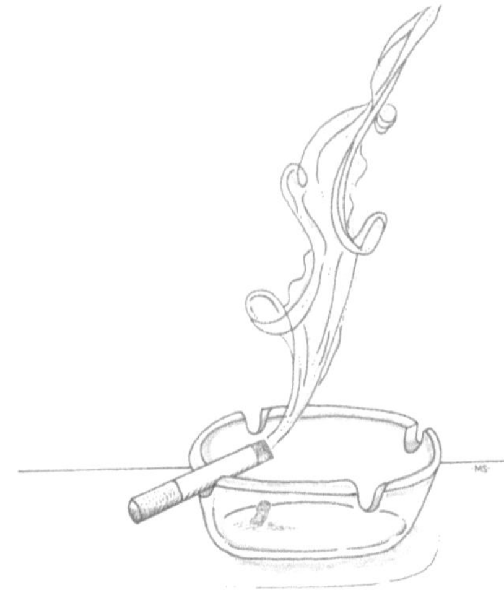

The Lion's Den

The walls trembled as shadows spiraled out of control. Daniel froze, tightly gripping his leatherback journal. The darkness was closing in. From above, he could hear the stone slabs of the estate crumbling. Soon, the Auttenberg House would fall apart, trapping Daniel beneath it. He exhaled heavily, sprinting up the next stairwell he could find, in hopes that this would be the last.

"Rebecca!"

His voice had grown hoarse from calling her name. Shoving the doorway at the top of the stairs open, Daniel peered through the empty darkness. "Rebecca?"

He grit his teeth together and trembled. This couldn't be. Surely he had checked every room in the estate; yet, Rebecca was nowhere to be found. Daniel cursed aloud, kicking the door.

"Goddamnit!"

He leaned against the wall before covering his face. His journal fell beside him, opening to a few written pages in the middle. Daniel cringed at the sight of the words and violently nudged the journal away.

"*This is all your fault*," he thought bitterly. "*If it weren't for you, Rebecca would still be here.*"

Daniel shook his head. How could he have been so selfish? All Rebecca wanted was for him to care and to be there for her – like a fiancé should. Instead, he hid in his fantasies, ignorant to her wishes and needs. And now, even Daniel was realizing this.

"*Selfish*," he thought, "*that's all I am.*"

Another page was full of writing before Daniel dipped his quill into the inkwell. His hazel eyes glinted in the faint candlelight, each sentence giving them more life than the last. This would be his final scene, when the notorious Adrian Auttenberg was dealt his death, and the hero escaped the forsaken castle.

"Adrian," Daniel said aloud with a laugh, "if there's one antagonist to ultimately stab you in the back, it'd be him."

The quill continued on, describing the final battle between Adrian and the hero. Daniel's blood boiled as it rushed through his veins, sparking and filling him with emotion. He smirked as he wrote, having the hero knocked down and ready to face Adrian's fruitless attack. He dipped the quill back into the inkwell before steadily removing it. Just as he was about to write again, a shrill voice echoed from downstairs.

"Daniel!"

A few drops of ink splashed onto his page, staining the once pure paper with their unintended marks. Daniel groaned, glancing at the clock. He was late again. He set his quill down before moving to the candle, snuffing it out. Heading for the doorway, he prepared himself for what was about to come.

Rebecca paced before the foot of the stairs, her black tea dress ruffling with each step she took. Her eyes met the ticking clock beside the stairwell, every passing minute causing her to sigh. She finally stopped pacing to fan herself. Her multiple layers were becoming warm, and her impatience wasn't helping. At the sound of Daniel finally approaching at the top of the stairs, she returned her flustered gaze.

"Daniel." She tried to keep her voice calm. "I thought we agreed to meet at the hour."

Rebecca motioned to the clock which now displayed half past. Daniel didn't acknowledge her as he made his way down the staircase. Rebecca folded her arms across her bodice, staring at him in intimidation.

"I got caught up in my work again," Daniel finally responded.

He slipped his coat on before adjusting it to his liking. Then, he moved to the buttons, slowly making his way from the bottom up as he closed it shut over his vest. Rebecca stared at him in disgust.

"Your work? It's *always* about your work, isn't it?" She moaned. "Daniel, can't you see there are things more important at times than your *work*?"

Daniel heaved a sigh. "I know what you're thinking, but the idea was there! I simply couldn't walk away from it."

Rebecca threw her arms into the air with a huff. "Couldn't walk away from it? You *promised* me, Daniel. You promised you would be down at the hour. That you wouldn't be late. That you wouldn't get caught up in your writings. And what do you do?"

"Sometimes petty things need to be sacrificed for those that are more important."

"I was just about to say the same," Rebecca murmured. "Do you *honestly* believe that your work is more important than my father's burial?"

Daniel remained silent.

"I can't believe you…"

Rebecca snatched her bonnet and placed it on her head. She took a deep breath and stared at the doorway. A few tears brought on by anger and betrayal built in her eyes as she parted her lips.

"For once, could you just think of me?"

"I do think of you, Rebecca," Daniel urged, only to have her shake her head.

"No… no you don't. That journal of yours, your imagination…your *fiction*… that's all that's important to you. And one day, you're going to realize that, but it will be too late. You can't hide forever in your fantasies, Daniel. Someday, they're going to hunt you down. Drag you into the darkness."

"You wouldn't understand. My imagination is my escape. To close your eyes and see a different world, why, it's magnificent. It could never destroy anyone. It's salvation! In fiction, I'm among friends, Rebecca."

"Friends…" She whispered, opening the doorway.

Her eyes met the carriage that had been waiting for them on the lawn. Sighing, she stepped outside the door.

"Just pray that those friends can save you the day the darkness comes."

Rebecca's heels clicked across the still damp ground from the rain shower the night before as she made her way towards the carriage. Daniel stood in the doorway, about to follow her out, only to be pulled back. A grin slipped across his lips as his eyes lit up. Leaning out of the doorway, he cried out to her.

"I'll be with you shortly, Rebecca! I have a marvelous new idea for a story!"

As he turned and headed back inside, Rebecca frowned. She glanced up to the carriage driver who turned back at her, questioning if she wished to wait for Daniel. She closed her eyes. Removing the ring from her finger, she set it on the empty seat beside her.

"No."

A crash echoed from outside the door as Daniel flinched. The stones were crumbling faster. Snatching the journal into his hands, he tugged the door open. A few chunks of the broken estate lay within the center of the floor. He stared at them in awe, finally hurrying out of the guest room and down the stairwell. The shadows crept in on him as he ran, reaching out for him with their long fingers. He knew it wouldn't be long before they snagged him, pulling him into the bowels of Hell. It's what shadows did, he thought to himself. Especially when they were in your mind.

Daniel spotted a large set of double doors at the end of the hallway, just beyond the shadows. He took hold of the handles, tugging harshly before stumbling backwards once the doors parted. He hurried inside, allowing his eyes to adjust to the lighting before proceeding. A chandelier lit the center of the room, revealing another set of stairs leading down to the main hall. As Daniel descended, his mind began to stir again.

His boots clicked across the stone floor as he gazed to the large windows that lined the open hall. Lightning flashed in the distance and rain pounded the glass mercilessly. Daniel stopped for a moment to watch and gather his thoughts.

"*The hall*," he thought, continuing to stare out the window. "*I'm certain I'm in the hall. If my assumptions are correct, then, the chapel should be nearby. That's where she'll be...*"

Daniel peered back through the dim lit hall before taking light steps as the wind outside howled. He could hear it batter against the large windows as lightning flashed. The white light illuminated the room slightly more, sending horrific shadows across the walls. Their arms stretched out for him, sharp toothed grins hungrily waiting for him to approach. From behind, they watched him with hollow eyes. Between the howling wind and pounding rain, Daniel could hear them hiss his name.

"*It's just in my head,*" he thought. "*A fantasy... like Rebecca always tells me.*"

His hand ran along the wall as he walked, corners becoming darker. The shadows were there, mocking him. He saw their grins, their vicious claws reaching for him. With every whisper, Daniel grew tenser. Finally, he shook his head.

"*No... this is all wrong! There aren't shadows here!*"

Daniel closed his eyes tightly, the shadows crawling towards him. They grabbed him with their snake-like fingers, tugging at his overcoat and tearing the fabric. More and more swarmed, circling him with their hellish shrieks. They engulfed him, clawing at him before Daniel gave in.

"No!" He hollered. "This isn't how it is!"

His eyes snapped open, the dark silhouettes retreating. Between heavy breaths, he glanced around the room, the sound of their cries replaced with music and laughter. Beneath the candles of the chandelier, the vibrant colors of young women's dresses flowed, contrasting with the shadows that swept across the walls. Daniel stood still, watching and listening to the couples as they twirled beneath the candlelight. He took a deep breath, peering through the crowd. Their whispers were soft, not like those of the shadows. Making his way out of the glittering palette of swirling colors, Daniel stood to the side, flipping open his journal.

"Dancing." He read aloud from the page. "Forever dancing in the Great Hall of Auttenberg."

Daniel slapped the cover shut again, gazing at the dancers. Masks covered their faces, keeping him from recognizing them; except for one. A woman stood on the opposite side of the hall, dressed in a flowing wedding gown. Her wavy locks of brown hair fell just at her shoulders, eyes irritated from crying. Her mask remained in her hands, allowing Daniel to get a better look at her face. Once their eyes met, he stammered her name.

"Rebecca?"

With that, she darted from the main hall and towards the doorway hidden in the darkness at the end. Daniel cried out for her again, pushing through the crowd. He chased after her, even when she vanished behind the door.

"Rebecca!"

The couples continued to twirl, as if nothing had happened. From the shadows of the room, a man stood. Watching. From behind his lion-faced mask, he smirked.

Daniel pushed the door open, calling Rebecca's name once more. The woman was nowhere to be seen, but Daniel continued on. There were no windows here to cast light. Just empty darkness.

"*The chapel should be at the end of the corridor*," Daniel thought as he steadily moved along.

His hand brushed against the wall as he walked, finally reaching the next doorway. He tugged it open, the light from the large windows catching his eye. Aside from the few pews and altar, the room mimicked the larger hall. It was still somewhat dark, but Daniel could make out shapes from the candles that lined the altar. Every few moments, the lightning would strike, as well. It was then, when the bolts ignited the room, that he saw it. Causing him to breathe heavily.

A lion statue stood hidden in the shadows, its mouth open and baring its large teeth. Its eyes glowed a deep yellow-green in each of the flashes, and Daniel couldn't help but back away. He placed a hand over his rapidly beating heart in an attempt to calm himself.

"*It's just a statue*," he thought, eyes still fixed on the stone beast. "*There's nothing to be afraid of. The story's ending... it's all been won. You know how it ends, Daniel. Stop worrying and find her!*"

The candles on the altar went out as Daniel froze in shock. The darkness crawled around him as he remained still, waiting for his eyes to adjust. He breathed uneasily, glancing down the aisle. With another crack of lightning, Daniel noticed something out of the corner of his eye that he hadn't before.

In the opposite corner of the room, propped against one of the pews was a pale white silhouette of a young woman. Cocking his head to the side, Daniel started over towards it, feeling his heart palpitate against his chest faster as he swallowed hard.

"Rebecca?"

His hands trembled as he reached out to touch her lifeless face. She was cold, and her body stiff. Her wedding dress was slightly torn, soaked in a deep red down her breast. Inhaling through quivering breaths, Daniel stared at her neck. Torn open and blood continuing to gush from it. His hands became covered in the warm fluid as he quivered. He pressed his head to hers, trying to swallow the tears and burning lump which formed in his throat.

"No…" He choked. "This isn't how it's supposed to be!"

He pulled her closer as the tears began to roll down his cheeks. Opening his journal once again, he flipped through the pages to find the last written chapter.

"He's supposed to find her alive... to save her. He's supposed to make it so the darkness could never haunt her again. He'd free her from the nightmare Adrian created. And they could live on together… forever…"

Daniel's shoulders quivered as his fingers bent the pages of the journal. His breaths became short and heavy, tears staining his cheeks. He simply couldn't turn another page. Rebecca's blood upon his fingers stained the pages and the sight of it caused him to violently throw the journal aside.

"This isn't how it was supposed to end!" Burying his face into Rebecca's hair, Daniel sobbed. "Oh, Rebecca… what have I done?"

The door creaked open as Daniel pulled his face from Rebecca's, peering over with misty eyes. Through the shadows, he saw the figure of a man approaching. He was dressed in his masquerade attire, lion mask covering his face. At first, Daniel didn't recognize him, but once he removed the mask, his eyes widened.

"Adrian?"

"I was wondering how long it would take you to catch on." The figure sneered.

"No," Daniel stammered. "This is impossible. You're… you're supposed to be dead!"

"Am I?"

Daniel sensed the mockery in his voice. "This isn't how it ends… you're supposed to be killed. The castle then starts crumbling and…"

"And then what? Your hero saves his wife-to-be?" Adrian motioned to Rebecca's lifeless body.

"Everything else was perfect… played out step by step… I don't understand. This isn't how the book ends."

"But it *is*, Daniel." Adrian grinned, yellow-green eyes glinting. "At least how you ended it."

"What?"

"You see, Daniel… you never finished your book. If you remember, you stopped writing before Rebecca's father's burial. After your little talk with her, you became so fascinated by your mind's newest creation, you never went back to what you were writing. Your hero never killed me; in fact, your hero never did anything!" Daniel shivered in rage as he glanced down to Rebecca, stroking her face once more. "But, now's your chance to change that. No one likes a story where the hero always wins, Daniel. You know how you want the story to really end. Not with the path of rose petals leading your hero and his bride home. No! You want there to be the trail of blood and my eternal living. Don't deny it. I know you've thought of it before. Even you know I was your greatest work of art."

"You bastard…" Daniel hissed.

"Isn't it a wonder what you can do with art, Daniel? You dream it to life."

"This isn't what I wanted."

"Sure it is," Adrian replied, grinning wider. "*You* imagined it."

Daniel closed his eyes tightly as he shook his head. "No…"

He continued to cradle Rebecca, even as Adrian took another step closer, staring down at the journal on the floor.

"You should have listened to your dear Rebecca. You do get caught up in your fiction far too much. It's taking over your mind. Dragging you to the darkness."

"No..." Daniel repeated softly.

"Ah, Daniel." Adrian sneered, watching the shadows as they crept across the floor, his eyes beginning to glint. "In fiction, you said you were always among your friends."

He steadily removed a dagger from the pouch at his side, silver blade sparkling in the flashes of lightning. The hilt matched the statues that surrounded the chapel: a lion's head with its teeth bared and eyes yellow jewels. Raising it, Adrian only beamed wider.

"But in reality, you'll find you're among lions."

ABOUT THE AUTHOR

Dorian J. Sinnott is a graduate of Emerson College's Writing, Literature, and Publishing program, currently residing in Kansas City, MO with his two cats. He enjoys traveling in his free time – especially to haunted locations. Dorian is a dedicated member of the Horror Writers Association and Horror Authors Guild. He is also the Editor-in-Chief at *Crow's Feet Journal*. Dorian's work has appeared in over 100 literary magazines and journals worldwide, as well as on podcasts and horror radio shows. His novel *It Came Upon a Midnight Clear* was nominated for the 2021 Eric Hoffer Book Award.

ALSO FROM DORIAN J. SINNOTT

IT CAME UPON A MIDNIGHT CLEAR

It's the most wonderful time of year – for everyone except Harold Trapp. With a tight deadline hanging over his head, stress is a frequent visitor, as are the two cats that mysteriously appear on his doorstep. But he soon realizes that there's something sinister hiding behind their sweet and furry demeanor.

AN ERIC HOFFER BOOK AWARD NOMINEE

Available now on Amazon!

AND FOR MORE SHORT HORROR…

INTO THE UNCANNY

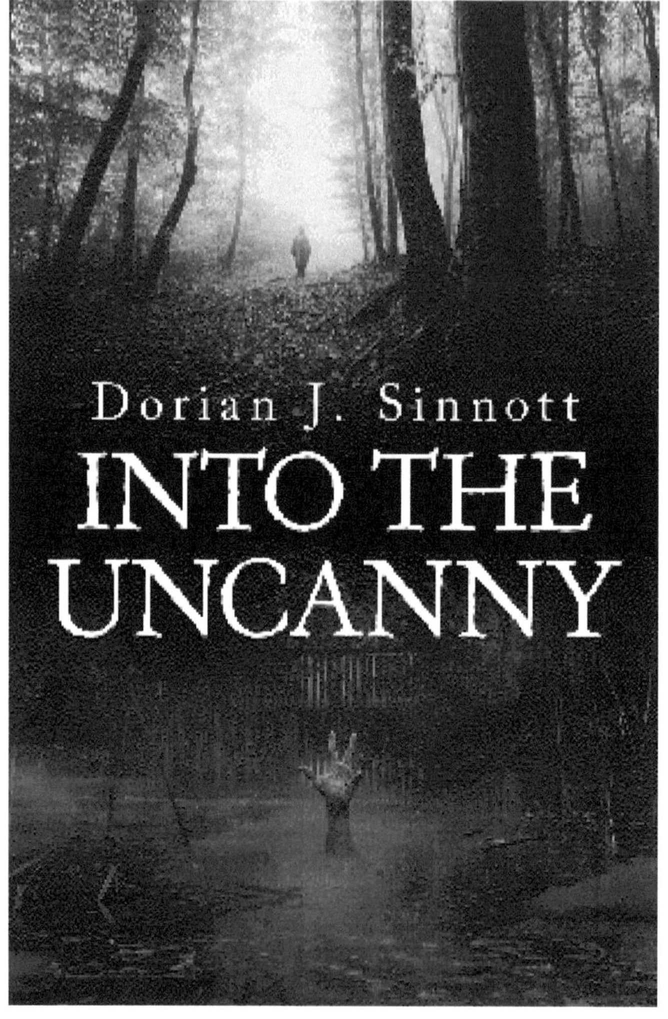

Available now on Amazon!

www.ingramcontent.com/pod-product-compliance
Ingram Content Group UK Ltd.
Pitfield, Milton Keynes, MK11 3LW, UK
UKHW041640190726
13854UKWH00006B/2604

9 798706 711627